I0781322

Atticus

Ravenwood Academy Book One

C. L. EASTON

Atticus

Copyright © 2023 by C L Easton

All rights reserved.

No part of this publication may be reproduced, distributed, or transmitted in any form or by any means, including photocopying, recording, or other electronic or mechanical methods, without the prior written permission of the author, except in the case of brief quotations embodied in critical reviews and certain other non-commercial uses permitted by copyright law.

Cover Design: Black Pirate Book Cover

Publisher: Black Rose Publishing

Ebook ISBN: 978-1-998910-05-2

Paperback ISBN: 978-1-990910-04-5

Playlist

"Let my heart be still a moment
and this mystery explore..."
-Edgar Allan Poe

Author Note

A little note from me to you. This is a piece of fiction. Take everything that you read with a grain of salt.

While you read Atticus, keep in mind that they are of age. Yes, they are stepsiblings. Yes, they do know what they are doing. That's why we enjoy it so much.

You are stepping into a why choose (reverse harem)

Object Insertion, Dub-Con/Non-Con, Virgin Female, Alcohol and Drug Abuse.

It does end on a cliff hanger. I'm sorry!

One

Jinx

Grovedale is the place to be if you want to further your education. Nope. Sorry, Ravenwood Academy is that place. Grovedale is the shithole town below RWA, where you go to die. I wanted to live, so I left and never returned. I never placed much thought into that town or the people living in it. I didn't want anything to do with those nightmares anymore.

Being here at Ravenwood has been a godsend from the first day. I felt a weight lift off my shoulders. It was only me and my cello and a sea of other students. I'll admit I was shy and lost when Dad dropped me off, and I was the odd one. The weird girl wearing all black that never grew out of the gothic-emo phase, and no one wanted to get to know me. Well, until a nerdy gamer named Spencer bumped into me.

Don't let the skinny jeans or band tees throw you off. This van-wearing gamer knows how to have fun outside of gamer land. We were meant to be best friends. I knew it, and he knew it. Since then, we haven't done anything without each other. And when I mean anything, I mean A-N-Y-T-H-I-N-G! Most of the ideas are Spence's, and I get to spend the time in the Deans' office trying to talk our way out of it. I wouldn't change a thing. It's been a dream being here with him. The only other downfall is that Spence doesn't leave his room much if it isn't to cause havoc or a party.

Summer is coming to an end, and school officially starts in a week. That means one thing—a big party at Cams. I dread going to this party, and Cam has a habit of coming on way too strong. I've been dodging his moves since the first year. I thought I had ditched him, but no such luck.

I'm still in my dorm, flicking through all my clothes, trying to think of something to wear when my bedroom door flies open.

"Seriously, Odette."

That's another thing. Spence here thinks it's hilarious to use my government name.

"Yes, Spencer Aaron Coldwell." I turn to look over my shoulder with a smirk when he walks into my bedroom.

"Oh, you bitch. I hate that fuckin' name." He moves to my bed, throwing himself onto it.

"Ya, well. I don't like Odette. Sounds like an old lady sitting in her rocking chair, knitting." I go back to sifting through my clothes.

"Wear the black skirt, with the black shirt."

I laugh. That describes my entire wardrobe. "Thanks for narrowing it down."

"I try my best, Jinx. Come on, we all know you'll wear your ripped skinny jeans, but wear that black corset thing and your leather jacket. You look bangin' in it."

I turn to face him. He sits up on his elbow, snaps his gum, and pushes up his glasses. "Spence, I don't feel comfortable wearing something like this to that party."

"Jinx, if you are worried about Clam Jam, I'll take care of him."

Ah, the secret nickname for Cam. We have a lot of code names for things around campus; it's one way we stay out of trouble with the swim team.

I grab the clothes Spence suggested, praying I'm not making the wrong choice. "I'll change, try to stay out of my snack cabinet."

Darrow Hall is where most students reside, with four co-ed floors; the best part of my dorm is that I'm the only one on the top floor—also known as the tower. I might also have the most oversized room, with my own kitchen and living space. My bedroom is separate, with an attached bathroom; I'm currently housed in changing into my outfit.

"Grab my boots for me, will ya?" I yell, throwing open the door. "Oh, and a pair of socks."

I touch up my makeup, then decide if I should leave my hair in a messy bun. I'm not going to impress Cam. Fuck him.

"Here, I picked a special pair for ya." His gray eyes sparkle behind his glasses.

I grab the socks, look down at them, and burst out in laughter. Eggplants and peaches. I think he's secretly trying to tell me something. Whatever, it's not like he's getting any peaches, either.

The August air is warm, a little too warm for my jacket. Spence wraps his arm around my shoulder as we stroll down the sidewalk. We passed a bunch of students who had arrived early or stayed behind. The first years have no idea what goes down here yet. Not until the first week, and we do a repeat. I've done two of these back-to-school parties. They get boring after a while and the fact that the swim team always puts them on. Pass.

The swim team has its own frat house on campus; the academy treats them like gold, and they can't do anything wrong. Blackwood house is next to the woods, and it's creepy as fuck. It is another reason I don't love coming here. At least Darrow is close to the main campus and in the open. Blackwood house is a cross between the Addams and Bates house. Tall, dark, and old.

Stairs lead up the small hill to the main door. The Queen Anne Style has always been my favorite. The turret gets me, probably because I live in one.

Walking up to the steps, beer cans already litter the front yard, a couple already making out, and I'm if I look close enough—yep, that's a penis in the vagina. Couldn't even find a room. Spence steers me to the front door, chuckling under his breath.

"Watch yourself, Spencer." I hiss.

"Odette, I swear. I'll get you drunk and film you doing the macarena."

I gasp. "I'll record one of your live streams and stream it to the whole school."

"Shit," he whispers.

I smile in triumph. He grabs the door handle, also smiling in triumph.

"Ready for Clam Jam?"

"God, I hate you." I adjust my fanny pack on my hip.

"You gonna be okay?" Spence looks at my fanny pack.

"I'll be good." Taking a deep breath. I wait for him to open the door.

The stench of booze lingers in the air when we walk in. We make our way deeper into the house, weaving in between bodies. By the time we reach the kitchen, I'm craving that drink, and so far, I haven't bumped into Cam.

I leave Spence to do his thing while I take stock of all the choices of liquor. The one thing about Blackwood is they never cheap out on the booze. On the floor sit two kegs. The kitchen island is covered in bottles of rum, vodka, and whiskey, and I'm sure there's more, but I can't tell. I grab a solo cup and a flavored rum. I learned not to mix these strongly a while ago, especially when horny boys are around.

I can honestly say that I am not having a good time. Spence is chatting up some chick with, and I'm saying this as nicely as I can. Big titties. That's all I can see; her dress is so low-cut that I'm surprised that her nipples aren't making an appearance like your period does when you aren't expecting it. My eyes just naturally drift to her chest. I can't help it. I'm sure Spence doesn't even know the color of her eyes, which are... Brown. At least I'll know, just in case he asks.

I'm minding my own business watching the group of bodies on the shitty dance floor grinding with each other when shivers roll down my back. I sip my drink, trying not to think about what's happening. Either way, the inevitable is coming across the kitchen, standing at six foot three, with dark brown hair that's always perfectly styled. Don't get me started on the khaki shorts and a white tank top he's wearing. He looks like a preppy douche. I try not to roll my eyes. Instead, I take another sip. The alcohol is already flowing through my system, and my tongue isn't going to hold back.

"Mmm, Jinx the minx. Looking lovelier than ever," he says as he nears me.

"Cam, wish I could say the same, but what's going on with." I wave my hand at his outfit. "This?"

He moves to my side, resting his hand on the counter behind my back.

"I didn't expect you to actually show up, thought my crowd was too good for you."

I shift away from him. "Oh, you aren't too good for me, but Spence wanted to come."

He scoffs. "That gamer nerd."

I can feel my blood boil. I look across the kitchen to see Spence staring at us. If you look closely, you might see his jaw clench. I close my eyes for a second, trying not to lose control.

"Cameron, only I am allowed to call him a nerd. If I hear those words come out of your mouth again, the entire swim team will discover that you like to shove foreign objects up your asshole."

I slam back my drink before dragging Spence onto the makeshift dance floor.

"Whoa, whoa. What's going on?" He tries to dig his heels in, and I pull him harder.

"It was either this or a glass going through a jugular. I figured this was the safest bet."

The beat of the music radiates off the floor all the way into my chest, making it hard to breathe. Bodies push against us, making me close to Spence. His hand wraps around my back, pulling me in tight.

"You know, this would be awkward if I weren't your bestie."

"I have no regrets about this. How did it go with big titties?" We move our bodies together with the beat of the music, and I'm so thankful that we are very platonic. Because if I had to feel his dick digging into my stomach, I'd probably junk-punch him.

He shrugs. "You know, I'm sure they were fake, and I'm an all-natural kinda guy. She did give me her number, so I might hit her up."

I roll my eyes; I knew he would. He can't resist the boobs. Spence leans down. His tall frame does a great job of hiding me most of the time.

"Clam Jam keeps glaring at me. Think he's jelly or something?"

"That dickhole can rot in the ground for all I care. I don't want to deal with another one of these parties unless it's life or death."

He cringes. "That bad?"

"The words nerd were exchanged. So yes. That bad."

I can feel his body tense. I grip his biceps, trying to calm him down. The one thing about Spencer is that his rage can get out of hand. I've been trying to help him not get into fights, but I could make an exception this one time. I release his arm and take a step back. The ball is in his court. He's old enough, or so I would hope so. He slowly smiles and nods.

I'm not going back to my room anytime soon.

Two

Jinx

I'm watching Spence standoff with Cam, and it didn't take long for him to cross the room once I told him. Whatever it was, either Cam calling Spence a nerd or trying to hit on me all night. Either way, this fight was coming. Except when Cam lands the first blow, I'm not having it. Spence doesn't deserve this. He might be a lot of things, but he is not a fighter. I wish he would learn.

The sad thing is Spence won't be winning. Cam will get his stupid friends to join, and it'll be over. He can never fight alone, and I can only do so much. The music stops, and all these kids that claim to be independent adults start chanting. I try to push my way through the crowd so I can kick Cam's ass myself. I end up elbowing big tit

McGee in the boob and silently cheer. Take them fake ol' titties home.

When I make it to the inside of the circle, Spence is already covered in blood, and it's dripping from his nose and mouth. Cam, on the other hand, looks perfectly fine. Heat flushes through my body, and my cheeks flame to life. I thought Spence had an anger problem. Well, I'm not far behind. I dig through my fanny pack, slipping on my skull ring. I may be five foot two, but I know how to punch. Cracking my knuckles, I lose it. My fist lands on Cam's face when he's not expecting it, and he stumbles back, leaving Spence alone.

"The fuck!" he yells, touching his cheek and coming back with blood on his fingertips. His wild eyes land on me.

"Cam, I think you've done enough." I pull Spence behind my back. I feel his body sag against me. I try not to move forward from the pressure.

Some of Cam's friends move behind him. Liam, Shane, and Emery. Like I said, he can't even finish a fight alone.

"Think your little boy band will help you, Cam? Seriously, can't you fight one fight alone?" I taunt him, knowing full well that he's getting madder. "Wanna fight me?"

He goes to make a move, but Liam grabs his arm.

"Are you fucking crazy? You going to hit a chick in front of all these people?" Liam hisses.

Cam yanks his arm free and points at me. "Watch your back, Jinx."

"Is it going somewhere that I'm not aware of?"

"Jinx shut the fuck up," Spence murmurs. He leans more onto my body, shifting me onto my right leg. I look up at his face and think otherwise.

"Fine, you need to clean that face of yours."

Spence chuckles. "Yeah, I probably look like a prized pig right now. That jackass never let me get one hit in. I had a whole plan, and he ruined it."

I pat his arm, shaking my head. "I'm sure you did. Let's get the hell out of here."

I flip the bird at Cam and steer Spence toward the exit. The crowd disperses, returning to drinking and whatever shenanigans they were up to. This party was shit, to begin with. When we finally make our way outside, Spence stands up straight.

"Are you kidding me? You faked it this entire time?"

He shrugs. "I was kinda over it, anyway. He would've kept wailing on me until I was on the ground, and I didn't want to fuck up my face any more than it is."

He grabs me by the arm, hauling me down the sidewalk. While I'm still processing the words he laid out, the ass was faking it. Honestly, I shouldn't be surprised he's been pulling stunts like this for years now.

"I can't believe you, you could've given me the secret wink, or I don't know anything before I went in guns a-blazin'."

"Yeah, well. I wasn't expecting the white knight to come in. So, that's all you, Teeny."

Ugh. I need to think of more nicknames for him.

"Spence, please tell me the next time you decide to fight somebody that you try to get at least one punch. Because now that I know your whole scheme, I'm staying out of it."

He exhales dramatically. I'm waiting for it.

"To be fair, I tried. Okay. But that asshole punched first, and then it went from there. I couldn't get my fist in anywhere."

I stop dead in my tracks. "Nowhere. You couldn't get a fist or a knee anywhere?" I raise my brows, shaking my head. "Not even the nuts?"

"Whoa, my dear. The nuts are always off-limits. Yeah?"

"Um, no. The nuts. Then when his head goes down, you fuckin drive your fist into his face. Okay. It's fighting 101." I shrug.

He blinks. "Who taught you how to fight?"

"It's facts for any woman out there. Duh."

He laughs nervously. "You know what? You fight how you need to, and I'll fight how I need to."

"You fight to lose, Spencer. I win. So, let me know how that works for you."

We continue our walk back to the dorm, and knowing Spence, he will stay in his room to game all night, the first years will be showing up either tomorrow or the next day, and I'm dreading it. I'll probably watch Spence stream while I practice my cello. I'm not one to game, but I do support my friend.

"Want me to walk you up?" He's holding his door open for his floor.

"Nah, go get your stream on. I'll join in later. Wash your face and place an ice pack on your lip."

He waves me off. "It's fine, besides. Chicks dig scars."

"I'll see you tomorrow. Go kill your little dudes in your game."

"That's not how it works, Jinx."

"Whatever," I holler over my shoulder. I walk up the last flight of stairs to the quietness. This is what I love the most.

Just me.

Unlocking my door, little taps come at my window. The highlight of my night has finally arrived. Crossing my room, I unlatch my window. My black feathered friend hops on my ledge.

"Hello, Edgar." I watch him hop onto my desk, where he knows I hide his treats. "Don't be a pig."

He makes a little kraa when I don't move fast enough. I found Edgar while walking home during the second week of my first year. When he was ready to fly, I had to let him go. But that damn Raven hasn't stayed away since. Not that I will complain; he's the cutest thing.

"Here, I have to practice." I hand him a few pellets of food before turning my computer on and grabbing my cello.

Gwah, Gwah. Edgar chants his thanks. I stroke the feathers under his chin. He wiggles his head around my finger. Such an odd duck he is.

"All right, mister, I need to practice. This is the year that I will land that solo, and if I start now, I will have a better chance at wooing Professor Von. I can feel it, Edgar."

Gwah.

It's all the support I need. Spence has already started his game. I'm not even sure what it is. I usually end up muting him when I practice. His chatting distracts me, and I end up paying too much attention to him playing.

I get lost in my music. Swaying back and forth to the music, this is usually the time my mind wanders.

I've been playing since Dad took me to the symphony, and my eyes landed on the largest instrument. Dad said if I could carry it, I could play it. Um. Turns out I couldn't carry double bass, so I settled for the cello. Even at eight, I struggled to carry it. That's where my height let me down.

I lost interest in music when I turned sixteen; boys didn't like a girl who played classical music. I wanted a boyfriend and to be what they were looking for. What a pipe dream, now that I think about it. That was also the year Dad started dating for the very first time.

While Dad's love life was flourishing, mine was dying. I didn't have much luck finding a boyfriend. I should've known better. What boy would want a girl that dresses weirdly, doesn't speak much, and when she does, it's telling them to fuck off. I might be a tad strong-willed. That's when I picked music back up. It was the summer before senior year.

The year my life went to the pits. Dad went from dating to marriage. I also went from being an only child to having two stepbrothers. I haven't seen them in three years.

My strings scratch against my bow. "Fuck." Just the thought of them messes me up. I see Edgar slowly make his way to the window. "You leavin' me?"

I rest the cello in its bag before walking to my window. With a hop, he's gone. Now, I'm not in the mood to prac-tice. I sit in front of my computer, unmuting Spence. His voice fills my small living space along with gunfire. Boys.

I love Spencer and all, but I'll never understand the games he plays. But the entertainment is worth it. I'm looking forward to this school year. Last year, and I'm finally free of this town and the boys that live below. I'm glad that they don't attend the same school as me.

I made Dad promise me that they go to community college, and for the last two years, it's been complete bliss.

Living with those twins was the worst year of my life. They made it a point to cause misery every day. Mainly Atticus.

Three

Atticus

I've been looking forward to this day since we learned we were no longer welcome back at Grovedale College. Ravenwood Academy will be my home for the following year. The only thing making it worthwhile is having Ashton and Maddox with me. I'm still not free from the one person who I hate the most. Considering he's the Dean of this place.

"So, how does this preppy-ass school even work?" Ashton asks from the back seat of Maddox's 67' Impala.

I look out the windshield as we get closer. The tall tower is the only thing you can see through the trees. I heard this place was built in 1820 and had significant upgrades. It's still creepy if you think about it. Since getting kicked out of Grovedale, we had no choice but to come here. It wasn't our fault, okay, maybe a little, but how would we know that fire would escalate like it had? I did. I set the fucking building on fire. Those cunts had it coming. You don't mess with Maddox and expect nothing from it.

"From what I was told, we all bunk with the swim team except Maddox. Lucky asshat." I take a deep inhale of my smoke.

He chuckles.

If I have a say, that'll be changing. No way in hell am I staying with my teammates for this entire time. I'll kill the pricks. I don't care who they are. I stick with Ashton and Maddox. They understand me. When the school comes into view, it blows me away.

"Holy shit, bro. This place looks haunted," Ashton says as he weasels himself over the bench seat, squishing between Maddox and me.

"One person haunts it, and I'm determined to find her."
Maddox chuckles again.

Entering through the steel gates. The main campus building looks ominous. The stone structure stands four stories high. Two grand torrents frame the main entrance to the building. It reminds me of a castle. It is fuckin' old.

"We need to see Prescott first and resolve our living situation," I say.

"Want me to come?" Maddox finally speaks.

I shrug. "Might as well. We plan on living with you."

Ashton wraps his arm around Maddox. "Aw, aren't you excited? You still can't get rid of us," he chirps.

"Yay," Maddox fakes his excitement.

Maddox pulls into the parking lot and parks his baby near the back. God forbid if anyone parked near it. He's been overprotective of his car ever since he bought it. I'll admit it was the best purchase any of us has made, and we've made some stupid purchases. Ashton decided he wanted a boat; we don't even live near water. He bought the boat anyway. That thing sat in the driveway for the longest time.

To this day, I have no idea what went through his head. Don't get high and buy.

On the walk to campus, we pass many people hauling their things into another stone building. That must be the dorms. My eyes draw upwards to the tower. It's impressive. The view must be insane. Whoever has that room is a lucky fuckin' bitch.

"Think we'll get our way?" Ashton doesn't look convinced as we enter the main building.

"No," Maddox grunts out.

"Thanks, man, thanks for all the encouragement. You just don't want to share your dorm with us." I pat his back.

He shrugs.

After much confusion, we find the administration's office. The décor in this place is very different. The floors sparkle in dark marble, and the main hallway is lined in black brick. If you didn't know better, you would think this was a church, not a school. I'm not sure what we got ourselves into.

The woman behind the desk reminds me of a hipster grandma. She's wearing a floral dress with a wide leather belt. The chunky glasses with a chain really sell it for me. Her gray hair swings as she types vigorously on her keyboard. I clear my throat to gain her attention. Her head snaps up.

"Oh, my goodness. I didn't hear you gentlemen come in." She wheels her chair closer to the counter. "I'm Florence, the secretary here at Ravenwood Academy. What can I do for you?"

I place on my most charming smile. "We need to see Dean Hawthorne."

"No appointment, I take it?"

"Um, stepsons. Does that matter?" Ashton interrupts.

Her eyes widen. "Oh, oh dear. Give me a moment." She slides her chair back and hustles away, disappearing into the back.

I turn to look at Ashton and Maddox. "Looks like we have status already."

Maddox hums. Okay, so Ashton and I have status. But Maddox is with us, so he gets what we get. It's been that way since we were teens. A power trio and no one messes with us.

"How long until this school figures out we are the new rulers?"

Ashton laughs. "Give it until morning. I'll make sure of it."

"Think you can work that fast? You hardly know the place."

"You don't need to know the place, brother. You need to know the right person. Find the nerd, scare the crap out of him, then he'll tell his friends." He smirks.

We may be twins, but we are so unlike each other. Don't let the blond hair fool you—we are no angels.

Florence bounces back into the office with a grin. "The Dean will see you now, head on back." She points to a hallway.

"Thank you, Florence, you've been a doll." I flashed her smile on our way past her.

Walking down the hall, we pass a few offices, but the one we need stands out the most. Black double wooden doors with gold ravens for door handles wait for us. Fuckin' classy ass.

I don't bother with knocking—after all, he's expecting us. Prescott's office isn't what I expected; it's bright and cheery. Gross.

"Ah, boys. I'm glad to see you made it here safe and sound. Sit."

I grab the seat in the middle across from him while Ashton and Maddox sit next to me. I stare at Prescott, waiting for him to say something, anything. It was his stupid idea that we attend this college. Community college was great and all, but. Well, we know that didn't work out in the end. This one had the swim team. The same swim team Ash and I had no choice but to sign up for in high school.

"I'm not living with my teammates," I tell him, keeping my face stone-cold.

He laughs. "Is that so." He loses all his niceness. "It's to be expected. You dug your grave, and now you shall live with your consequences. You two made it evident to become delinquents who wouldn't see reason. I gave you the option, and this is your choice. Just because you're both twenty now doesn't mean you're adults. I still rule you. This is my school." He tosses three folders onto the table.

"Maddox will be housed in Darrow Hall while you two lucky bastards are off to Blackwood House. Don't fuck it up. Cameron is the captain of the swim team. He'll set you up. Good day, gentlemen."

"The fuck," Ashton says. "Don't we get a say? We had to come to this shitty school on your terms."

"Guess next time. You'll listen to my rules." Prescott points to the door, dismissing us.

I grab the folders off the table. "You might think you rule this school, but you won't rule us. We aren't at home anymore."

Leaving the office pissed off. I do make sure to smile at Florence.

Ashton pushes open the main door complaining, "What a cunt. He could've said yes."

"Do you think we're going to listen? Maddox, we're moving in."

He groans. "I wanted to be alone."

"Sorry, man. It'll never happen. Not until Prescott figures something else out. When that happens, we're in your room."

I watch as Maddox's shoulders slump. I get it, and he needs his personal space. He's been like this since we've known him. He's a very private guy. Letting anyone in is hard for him.

"Might as well grab our bags and move in. I'm sure Prescott will figure it out in a matter of hours. That Cam dude will be calling once we don't show."

Ashton rolls his eyes, and I feel he won't be getting along with our captain. The thing Ashton hates the most in the world is a nark.

I light another smoke as we walk back to the car. It's one of my guilty pleasures. I'm unwilling to give up; I like another pleasure too, but I need to find her first. With the way everyone is showing up, I don't have hope of finding her today. Slamming the trunk of Maddox's car, we haul our bags toward Darrow Hall.

"What do we know about this dorm?" Ashton asks, looking up at the tower.

"Fuck if I know, technically, this is Maddox's place." I open the folder with his name on it. "The Darrow Hall houses up to four hundred students at Ravenwood Academy. The student lounge features a historic fireplace, big screen TV, and a pool table. On-site laundry facilities are in the basement."

Maddox whistles.

"No shit, buddy. I wonder what the rest of the school is like. What room are we headed to?" Ash asks.

I look for some sort of keycard but can't find one. Huh, it seems like it's all digital. I see the passcode and room number. 410. At least we don't need to make keycards for each other. I'm surprised this place upgraded to the twenty-first century, on a few things, that is.

"Elevator?" I ask once inside the building.

Ashton shakes his head. "Nope, start climbing." With a tug, he adjusts the bag on his shoulder. He starts first, and we follow. Maddox still doesn't say anything. If he does say anything, he'll end up bitching us out.

The fourth floor isn't anything I would scream home about. I am surprised it has vending machines tucked next to the exit. Good to know, especially when I have late-night cravings. I smile as a group of girls pass by. A co-ed building. Interesting. It's a weird bunch of people that attend this school. Mostly elite gifted people.

Opening the door to our place, my first impression is Prescott is sucking up to Maddox. He gave him a fuckin' suite.

"Jesus, you have a fucking kitchen and living room in here. How is that fair." Ash pushes his way into the dorm room, throwing his bag onto the couch.

Maddox walks around his new place, shrugging his shoulders. "It'll do. Where are you two sleeping?" He casually strolls to the only bedroom.

I guess I didn't think of this. *Shit.* Ugh. Looks like Prescott won again. Fucker. He knew all along that we wouldn't be able to live with Maddox. If he wants to make my year a living hell, I can make his one too. He forgets who he's dealing with. We've only been living with him for three years, and I know all of his secrets, which he doesn't want anyone to discover.

I look over at Ashton. He's lounging on the couch, relaxed as ever. I hate to break it to him, but for now, I guess Prescott wins. That is until our new housemates discover how annoying we can get. I'll get my way.

"Let's go. We'll leave Princess Buttercup here alone." I grab my bag, tossing Maddox his folder. He better not get too comfortable. We'll be visiting all the time.

"Ah, man. I was about to fall asleep. Our teammates better not be dickholes." Ashton grabs his bags, moving to the door. "Enjoy the peace and quiet, Mad."

We're silent as we descend the stairs, not that we have to talk much—our bodies do it for us. It's saying we are not impressed with this shitty outcome. It was my first day here, and I already wanted to commit murder, and then I saw *her*.

Walking across the campus, dressed in a black dress with slits on both sides, not stopping until they meet mid-thigh. Her hair has grown out since I've last seen Jinx, and fuck me, she's beautiful. She throws her head back, laughing at something the guy beside her says. Then I see it. His arm wrapped around her shoulder, guiding her along with him. Who the hell is this? I'm ready to fuck him up when Ashton holds me back.

"Not yet, brother. We need a game plan first. We can't do anything in public for the first time."

I shrug out of his grip. "Fine." I grit out. "I'm not waiting long until I get her alone. Sooner or later, she's mine again."

Going on three long years, I've been waiting. I'll be counting down the days until I get you, Jinx.

Four

Jinx

It's the day students move in. I would feel sorry for them, but I don't. I made one rule with the dean. No one moves onto the fifth floor with me. I need isolation. Also, who wants to hear the musical talents of a cellist? Fucking no one. It's loud and annoying, and I sometimes can't stand myself.

Spence mentioned heading down to the food court before all the newbies scout it out. I do need to stockpile my cabinets. That way, I don't have to eat down there. That involves me bribing Spence to take a drive into the city. I know exactly how to get my way.

It's so warm outside; maybe a cool shower will help. I throw my hair into a bun before stepping into the shower stall. I would wash it, but the thought of drying it. I couldn't be bothered. A quick washdown is all I've got in me this morning. Heading to my closet, I grab the first black dress I find.

Me: Ready? I'm just getting dressed.

Pencil: Yeah, I need some more time, you know how to get in

Me: Lazy ass.

Pencil: It was a late night

That's what he gets for shooting his little digital players. He'll never learn then again; I also encourage his behavior. I'm that kind of friend, though.

Swiping my bag off the back of my couch, I slip my combat boots on. Not bothering to tie them, I can do that when I get to Spence's place. Climbing down the stairs to the fourth floor, chatter can already be heard from students arriving—the option to stay all year if you're an older student is available. The room you have is yours until you graduate. The dean is a hard ass about switching rooms. He rarely does it.

Spence's dorm is at the end of the North Hall, room 409. He has the best view, or so that's what he likes to say. It faces the track, and he only likes to watch the girls run. Glad I was blessed with small boobs. Without knocking, I entered his code and was instantly greeted by a bare ass.

"For fuck's sake, Spence. You knew I was coming. Get some clothes on." I slap a hand over my eyes. I don't need to see some things, and my best friend's nakedness is one of those things.

"Didn't think seeing me would make you come, Teeny." He laughs.

"Gross, you make me dryer than the desert. Clothes. Now."

"Yeah, yeah. Don't get your panties in a wad."

I hear his feet shuffle out of the room before I lower my hand. Guys, ugh. Now, I need to find the Lysol and clean all the surfaces before I sit down.

"Better?" Spence walks out in black jeans and a band tee and holds his checkered Vans.

"Yes, was that so hard to do in the first place?"

He tilts his head and smirks. "Spencey here needed to feel the fresh air before being couped up for the day." He points to his dick.

"Gross, Spencer. You owe me and my eyesight now." Perfect, now I won't need to bribe him.

"Why?" He narrows his eyes, moving closer to me. "Where am I taking you?"

I shot him my best dazzling smile. He only shakes his head.

"That won't work on me. The Jinx I know doesn't fuckin' smile." He walks to his fridge, opens it, and grabs a water bottle. He looks at me, and I shake my head.

"Oh, come on. I need to stock my cabinets with snacks; you know I don't have a car. I'll buy you that game you want."

He drinks his water, never taking his eyes off me. With a final huff, he caves. I knew he would; he definitely wants that game.

"Fine, but we buy it first, then your stupid snacks. But I still want to hit up the food court."

I roll my eyes, nodding my head. "I wouldn't deprive you of your food."

———

August heat and black clothes don't get along—another reason why Autumn is the superior season of all time. Because walking across the courtyard, I'm already melting, having Spence walking with his arm wrapped around my shoulder doesn't help.

"All right, Jinx sauce, I need real food once we get into the city. This college food is bad for my taste buds."

I can't help but laugh. "Such a drama queen, aren't you? The food isn't that bad."

"That's because you can't taste anything anymore."

I pull away from him. "Mmm-hmm, and what can you taste all mighty one?"

He looks at me and smirks.

"Leave the pussies out of it. It's a topic I don't want to know about. Can't you talk about that with your guy friends?"

He expands his arms. "What, guys, Jinx? Do you see them? I don't, so you get to hear about my nights in puss town."

"Nope, I don't tell you about dick town."

He chuckles. "Have you ever been to dick town?"

I huff. "Nunya business." I walk away from him. That's a touchy subject, and I don't think I need to open it up again. The douchebag knows the reasons behind it.

"Wait, I didn't mean it." His big arm wraps around my waist. "I swear, forgiveness?" Those puppy dog eyes come out behind his glasses, and I cave.

"You dick, hurry up. I'm already finished with this stupid day." I could feel eyes on me the entire time we walked across the yard. Shivers roll down my spine, and it's the same feeling I had all those years ago. But it's gotta be from all the new students looking at the goth girl for the first time. It's all in my head.

"Jinx, you doing all right?"

I shake my head. "Yeah, let's get you fed."

Entering the food court, we scan our student food card. Every month, it's loaded with a monthly allowance. I think it's bullshit, like most things on campus. One other way for this school to control their most elite students. If you look closely in the deep dark corners, you'll find some culty shit going on. After all, only the most talented people are accepted here.

Even when I am eating now, I can feel the same sensation as I did earlier. While Spence talks, I take that time to scan the surrounding tables discreetly. Nothing. Whoever it is, is keeping to the shadows or is behind me. I'm sure if I kicked Spence out of his spot, he would start questioning me. I picked a good day to get out of here. Too many people are beginning to fill the small area, sending my heart rate up.

"Ready?" Spence asks. It's almost like he can sense my discomfort.

"Please, I'm so ready for the city. It's been too long."

"Well, that's because I hate going. But since I'm nice and school is starting, we won't have many more chances to leave. You'll be knee deep in your cello."

I glare as I stand. "I'm getting that orchestra slot, so deal with never seeing me once school starts."

"I'll be your hype man either way and if you don't get in, I'll be the first person going postal on your stupid music teacher's ass. He's a dick and should've given you that spot last year."

"Yes, well, I guess Piper was doing more than playing the piano. Because she was horrible." I might still be a bit saucy about it. It should've been my spot. I worked so hard last year. I attended every practice, concert, and whatever else Professor Vos handed me. But none of that mattered since he was fucking Piper. Now that she's graduated and gone, I have a chance.

***

"Do you seriously need all of this?" Spence holds up my fifth bag of chips.

"Uh, yeah. I do. Why you being so judgy? I don't judge your food purchases. Mister, I need boxes and boxes of candy."

Spence sticks his tongue out. "It's for when I stream."

"How original. Any other lies you wanna spill while you're at it?" I throw another bag of chips into the basket. Spence laughs from behind me.

I hold up my finger, silencing him.

I won't lie; shopping with Spencer is nice and all. But I wonder what it would be like to shop with a girl. Making friends with girls has always been tricky. They always saw me as the weird outcast and didn't want to get mixed up with that.

I drowned myself in music and books, well, except for when I tried to get a boyfriend. If not for leaving and coming to RWA, I wouldn't have met my favorite nerd. It's just I want to experience some things without a male around all the time. I don't know how to interact with them.

It has always been Dad and I growing up until he re-married, but I didn't spend time with his new wife even then. She's too arrogant for me. We clashed the moment she moved in. Another reason I never go home for visits is because her entitlement gives me a headache. How her sons turned out the way they did is still impressive, not that they are angels beyond any means. Lord knows Atticus is a fucking psycho. Not in the *I'll murder you in your sleep sort of way*—more like *I need you and won't stop until you're mine.* He might murder you, I'm not sure, to be honest.

That's why I made it a point never to go home. When the guys said they were going to community college and not going to RWA, I decided it was best to stay in the school's safety. I don't need them anywhere near me. It was bad enough living with them for a year.

It was complete torture when they moved in with Dad and me. It wasn't as bad when Maddox was around, but I barely made it through high school with them. I can't imagine them being in the same school now.

Five

Jinx

Four Years Ago

I'm sitting in the backyard with my favorite cello practicing when Dad steps outside. He has that look, one that I won't be excited when he tells me whatever news he has.

"Hey, sweetheart, how's the music coming along?" He takes the seat next to me, waiting until I pack away my instrument.

"What's up, Dad?" I turn to face him.

I watch his brows furrow. "Well, you know how I went out on a few dates and all?" He looks at me, and I nod. "Okay, good. I—we got married."

"Married? Legally?" I ask, confused.

"Yep, no other way these days."

"Do you even know this person? It's rather sudden, don't you think? And why now? After all these years?" I asked him all the questions he didn't think about. He's old. Why would he think of these?

He inhales deeply. "Odette. It's been eighteen years. I still love your mother, but I need to move on. I can only hope you support my decision because it involves you, too. I want you to be happy."

"I am, Dad. If you're happy, I'm happy."

He pats my back. "Okay, good, because she has two sons, and they are moving in tomorrow." He gets up and leaves.

"Whoa, wait." I scramble out of my seat, rushing after him. "What do you mean she has two sons? You can't lay that on me and then leave."

"Their names are Atticus and Ashton."

"Age? I'm not living with babies."

"They aren't babies. They are the same age as you. They start the senior year, and I was hoping you could show them around the school."

I dropped my head. "Dad." I groaned. "Please don't make me do this." I look up at him.

"Sorry, sweetheart, but it's a new school for them. They'll need someone to show them around."

"You aren't leaving me with much time, are you? Couldn't bring them by before you married her?" I play with the hem of my shirt. "I'll do this because I love you."

He kisses me on the forehead. "I know. I love you too."

———

My leg won't stop bouncing; it's anticipating when these teenage boys will walk through the front door. Dad is busy in the kitchen prepping lunch; it's like he's all domestic now that he's married. I don't know how to handle him. When the doorbell rings through the house, he's running like a chicken with its head cut off.

"I got it, don't worry. Don't say anything mean."

I place my hand over my heart. "I would never." Out loud, that is.

I've met Serena before, but I still loathe her. Nothing has changed. Her blue eyes still remind me of a money-hungry snake. This time, when she walks into the house, she clings to Dad, and I need to hold back the bile that rises in my throat. Snake.

"Mom, where do you want these bags?"

My gaze swings to the open door where a tall blond boy stands, holding three suitcases. Behind him stands another blond. Holy crap. I have to deal with twins, but not just twins. They have to be hot, too. Shit.

"Oh, um, Prescott, hunny, where should the boys put their things?" Serena's nasally voice radiates through the room.

"Odette can show them to their bedroom, can't you, sweetheart?" Dad looks at me, narrowing his eyes, telling me not to say anything but to go along with his words.

"Yes, Dad, I would love to show them," I answer sweetly. For an added touch, I flash him a smile.

I head for the stairs, not waiting for the double A's. Their grunts and groans follow behind me as they struggle to haul their things up the stairs.

"Can you slow down?"

"Seriously, what's the rush?"

I look over my shoulder. "I do have better things to do than babysit you two. Starting tomorrow, I need to show you around. It's bad enough that you're taking over my house. Now you're taking over my school."

I'm not sure which one it is, Atticus or Ashton, but they laugh. "Oh, don't be like that. Do you think we want to be here? Our shitty mother only wants your dad for his money. Don't let her fool you."

"News flash, every woman wants my dad for his money." I point to a door. "That's your room. You'll have to share."

"Don't worry about us sharing, Odette."

For just meeting me, he's a condescending jerk.

When Maddox bought his car, that's when everything started. Atticus is the ringleader, while Ashton goes along. The night that they broke into the school was the last straw. I swear Dad was ready to ship them off to boarding school if they didn't clean their act up.

"Figure it out, boys, swim team, or you're gone," Dad tells them.

"That's not fair," Ashton argues. "We had a good reason to break into the school."

"Whatever it was, it clearly was a stupid move. I hope it was worth it."

Atticus scoffs. "Like you would know if something was worth it." He stares at me while he says it.

I've noticed things with the twins. Lately, I thought it was just my imagination, but occasionally, I catch Atticus staring at me. It unnerves me how he can crawl under my skin. Atticus is very intense when he talks; his bright blue eyes lock onto yours when he speaks, and he never does something without reason. Ashton, though, is easy-going and so laid back. When you're feeling down, he'll joke with you. But don't let that fool you. I've seen him knock someone out because they bumped into him.

"I'm positive we did it for a reason, Prescott," Ashton states, looking at me too.

I keep quiet. It was a deal. No matter how much my mouth wants to run, I clamp it shut. I didn't think Dad would go this extreme with a punishment—he never has in the past. That's why I asked them to do what they did.

"That's enough. I'll give you the night to think of what you want, but you two must clean up your act." With his final statement, he leaves the living room.

"I should just tell him," the words fall out.

"Don't even, Jinx. You asked for a favor, and we followed through. You know the deal. You owe us one."

I watch as Atticus leaves.

"You know he'll want what's owed to him, Jinx," Ashton whispers. "He isn't one to wait, either." He leaves me, too.

I knew better than to ask them, but I was desperate. I had no one else, and they've become popular since they started school. Everyone wants to be their friend. That only brought on the mean girls asking about the Banks brothers, and when I wouldn't give them the answers, my things started to go missing. But when my cello was stolen from the music room, I lost it. I couldn't find it, so I confronted the twins, asking them.

Atticus had one request. Me. The one thing he wants and can't have and will never have. I agreed only so I could get my cello back. That's the only thing I cared about, and I can worry about my deal later. I don't think he'll want me. Besides, what do I have that he wants? He has the entire female population at school.

The twins have a swim practice tonight. I've been able to dodge every single one all year only because I've been trying to dodge the twins and Maddox. Unfortunately, my luck ran out. Dad and Serena are dragging me along. It's the only night I'm not knee-deep in music, and *family comes first*.

Only two more months, then we graduate, and I'm gone and never coming home. It's getting out of hand. I've been able to avoid Atticus every chance I have, but I can tell he's getting annoyed. He started smoking, going out more, and bringing girls home.

That's when I pulled away from hanging out with them. As much as I loved hanging out with Ashton and Maddox, I can't be around someone who smokes. He knows my health is more important but doesn't care anymore. I don't matter to him, and it hurts in a way.

Walking into the aquatic center, I'm greeted with warmth and a chlorine smell. My throat tightens, and I take a few deep breaths while I follow Dad to the bleachers. If I don't need to dig my inhaler out, the better. I can usually work through my triggers. I pat my fanny pack for reassurance.

Dad glances at me with a tight smile. "Doing all right?"

I simply nod. I stare back at the pool, waiting for what I'm not sure of. I don't even know what to expect. When I feel a body sitting next to me, I know it's Maddox.

"Hey, Maddox."

"Hey, Jinx," he mumbles.

We don't need to exchange words to understand each other; we just do. Maddox knocks my knee with his to gain my attention and points to the changing room. The twins walk out wearing dark gray track pants and an unzipped hoodie, showing off their muscular stomachs. My stomach twists in knots. Seeing them both walking out laughing and having a good time stirs something deep within me. Thinking of them that way shouldn't be allowed. They are my stepbrothers. I can't—won't think about them any other way.

I'm still watching when Atticus lowers his pants, revealing his blue Speedo, followed by Ashton. *Sweet baby Jesus.* I watch Ashton throw his head back, laughing at his teammates as he folds his pants and removes his hoodie. When I revert my eyes, Atticus is watching me. His usually bright blues have darkened. That cocky smirk appears as he hooks his hands into his waistband. I'm too far gone to look away. I keep watching as his fingers glide down his toned thighs. When I snap out of it, he gives me a wink.

"He'll never stop, you know that, right?" Maddox says.

I pull my gaze toward Maddox. "I have a plan. No need to worry about me."

"Mmm, I wouldn't bank on that, Jinx. I've known him for a long time. Atticus doesn't' mind sharing, but he wants what he wants."

"I'm not a plaything that he can share, Maddox." I stand to leave.

"Where are you going?" Dad asks. "It hasn't even started yet."

"The ladies' room. I'll be back before they start." I need a breather is what I need. I take the long way around the pool, away from the twins. I can feel their eyes on me until I step into the hallway. The cool air sends goosebumps along my skin. It's still not enough; I need to get further away.

I end up in the music room. Where else would I go? I don't have my cello, but somebody left their double bass. I'm not the best, but when in doubt. The somber sound fills the empty room. That's one thing I love about the bass: its dark sound. The sound of a guitar makes me skip a string.

Maddox. I should've known he would follow.

"Keep playing." He strums on his guitar, and the song I love by *Nirvana* fills the room. I get lost in the way he plays. I never understood why he never took music; he would be amazing in this class. After we finish playing, he moves closer.

"Maddox, you truly are gifted, you know that?" I watch as his hazel eyes brighten. His hand cups my face, and an unfamiliar tenderness sweeps through me as his thumb brushes over my bottom lip. "Maddox," I whisper. I cup his hand, squeezing as I lower it.

He nods with closed eyes. "It's not only Atticus or Ashton that want you, Jinx," he said, his voice falling to a whisper at the final word.

"I don't understand why me?"

"One day, you'll figure it out." He holds his hand out for me. "We need to get back to watch the boys. They'll be mad if we miss them."

One day? What the hell does that mean? Maddox doesn't wait for me. He grabs my hand, dragging me out of the music room. I dig my heels in, pulling my hand back. I hear him huff, and the next thing I know, I'm thrown over his shoulder.

"Put me down. This isn't fair, you ass."

"Don't be so stubborn."

I go limp, look at my finger, and grin with a quick jab into his ribs, causing him to stumble.

"Jinx, fuck. Don't touch me like that."

He throws me back onto my feet, his chest raising rapidly, eyes wide.

"Shoot, I'm sorry, Maddox. I didn't mean to hurt you." I go to touch his shoulder, and he jerks away.

"We need to get moving."

Without words, we walk together back into the aquatic center in time. I stay close to the door as Atticus dives from the board, slicing through the water like a torpedo. Never in my life have I seen someone swim so fast before. In a blink, he's back at the beginning. He rises out of the water like some god. Water drips off his muscular body, and I greedily watch it drip beneath his Speedo.

"Seems like you want him too," Maddox says, nudging my arm.

Sometimes, what you want isn't always what you can have. That's why I need to stay away.

Six

Jinx

The weekend before classes start, and the talk around campus is, obviously, Cameron's famous stupid party. This will be the biggest one of the year, considering all the students have officially moved in, making my life hell. I'm thankful for my room, but I give it half the year, and most of these kids will drop out. RWA may look like it'll be an easy place, but if you want to reach the top, you work your ass off. It's the only way to advance in this school. Unless, of course, your Piper, you sleep your way to the top.

Pencil: Guess what tonight is?! And yes, we are going, so don't even try to get out of it.

Me: Spence, please no. Remember the last party?

Pencil: My face healed up nicely. I have you to save my ass. Secondly, I have to find big titties again and get a rematch.

Ugh! I should've known this was coming.

Pencil: You owe me.

Me: How? I bought you that game you wanted.

Pencil: I'm sure you'll ask for another favor so I'm cashing in early.

Damn him.

Me: Fine.

Pencil: That's what I thought, Teeny.

That's it. Spence owes me one for once. When big titties turns into a stalking psycho, and he needs help, I'll take my dear ass time fixing that problem. Spence needs a lesson, and I'll dish it out.

Gwah.

I look up from my paperwork sitting on the desk to see Edgar on the window ledge. Oh, my beautiful feathered friend. Always showing up when I need him.

"Hey, sweet boy, ready for your treats? I know that's the only reason you stop in."

Gwah. He hops over to where his treats are and ruffles his feathers before diving in.

"Slow down. There's plenty." I laugh when he chows down like he hasn't seen food in weeks. "All right. School is starting on Monday, and with that, I'll be a little busy. I might not be around to give you a treat."

Edgar turns his head as if he can understand me.

"Anyway, I am being dragged to yet another party at Clam Jams. Too bad I can't get you to shit on his head. It would make my day, Edgar."

Gwah.

I stroke his head. Yeah, talking to a bird would classify me as insane. But technically, I have a human friend, so I'm doing all right. I watch as Edgar takes off, leaving me alone once again. I finish filling out my paperwork before I head for the bathroom. I'm not one to get all girly, but I'll do it with a bang if I have to go to this party again.

———

This time, I knocked on Spencer's door. I don't need another dick show. If gaming doesn't work out for him, he could make it as a stripper. I'm leaning on the doorframe, waiting for him to answer. That dick better not be jerking off.

"Spence, stop jerking off and open up." I knock again louder this time.

The door flings open fast, causing me to fall forward. Spence catches me. "Hey baby, I knew I could make you fall for me."

"Haha, you're a funny guy." I straighten up. "What the hell took you so long."

He takes the time to look over my outfit choice, and a low whistle is all I get. "Fuck Teeny, what are you trying to do tonight?"

I wore my leather skirt and a sheer mesh black bodysuit showing off my black bra. To top it off, I'm wearing my black pumps.

"Too much?"

Spence swallows hard, shaking his head. "No, not at all. I've never seen you look this gorgeous before. But, um, where's the fanny pack?" He spins me around.

"I'm praying that I won't need it."

He sighs. "Jinx, you're going to a party with all your triggers. Think it's a smart idea? Go strap that sexy little harness on with one of your bags, and you'll still look baggin'."

"You sure?" I look down at my outfit, rethinking my decision.

"Trust me. I am a man, after all, Jinx." He wiggles his brows.

Why can't I have it as easy as Spence? His easy fashion is what I want: jeans and a tee. Why must I try to impress people all the time? I know why; it's because who wants to befriend the weird goth chick? In the far corner of my brain, I still want more friends, even though I know Spencer is enough.

"I'll wait till you're done, and we can head back up together."

He shrugs, moving further into his room. "Pre-drinks?"

"Fuck it, pour it up." I head to his computer, turning on his music. The song instantly makes me shake my booty. I shimmy over to Spence, grab my drink off the counter, and take a sip while dancing.

"Oh, Teeny, I love you." Spence laughs as he joins me.

"You are simply jealous of my booty moves." He grabs my waist as we move as one.

"Yes, that's *totally* what it is. You're gonna be my wingman, right?"

I roll my eyes. "When am I not? Should we make a drink to go?"

You can hear the music down the street from Blackwood House, and this is my last time coming here, I swear. If it wasn't for Spence and his desire for big titties, I could be curled up under my blanket watching a horror movie.

"Drinks first, Teeny, then you can shake your ass again. Maybe I'll find big titties again."

"You know, Pencil. You should find out her actual name." I sigh, pushing the front door open. Sweat and beer are all you can smell in the air. Bodies pressed close together as we push our way to the kitchen. So far, I haven't seen Cam, and I love it. I sway with the music as Spence makes my drink.

"Having fun, Teeny?"

I give him a smirk. "It's not bad this time around. Ready to hit the dance floor, or we looking for your dream girl first?"

He shakes his head. "This would be easier if you were a dude. Come on, bring your drink. The last thing I need is for someone drugging you."

I pat his cheek, always looking out for me. I pass him, elbowing someone on my way to the makeshift dance floor.

"Watch it, Jinx."

That voice. I haven't heard in almost three years. I look back, meeting hazel eyes. Maddox. I want to stare more, but Spence won't let me linger. Something is different with Maddox. He isn't the same boy I left behind. But if he's here, that also means one thing. Atticus and Ashton are near.

"What's wrong? You look like you've seen a ghost?" Spence asks once we reach the dance floor.

"You could say that my past has caught up with me." I chug the rest of my drink, tossing the cup on the floor. That's Cam's problem.

"You doing all right?"

I wave him off. That's a problem for another day.

"Oh, I did see big titties earlier, so my plan is—"

"Spence, seriously, get her name." I interrupt.

His hand wraps around my waist, pulling me closer. "Clam Jam has officially arrived," he whispers next to my ear.

"Ugh, for once. Can he not show up?"

He dips me, and I get an upside view of the room. That's when I saw her. I tap Spencer's forearm, and he swings me up fast. The room spins, and I grab tight so I don't fall.

My stomach revolts. "Oh shit, gonna be sick." I swallow. "Big titties is over there." I point behind me.

He holds me steady. "You good?"

I wave him off. "Yeah, I'll be fine. I'll be in the kitchen after I use the bathroom. Go make your move, hotshot. This time, hold on to her phone number."

I'm usually pretty good at not overdoing it on my alcohol, especially at parties. More so, Cam's parties, I can't let my guard down around him. Ever since the first year, he's been trying to claim me. Like I'm a fuckin' puppy. He even went as far as switching his biology class. I tried bringing it up to my dad since he's the Dean, but it was pointless. There wasn't anything he could do. Cam is a sweet talker.

The only one that believed me was Spence. That's why he always sticks by my side. I also don't trust Cam with Spence alone, or I would never have come here. I know Cam has been out for his blood ever since the fight. I need to keep Spence distracted for the night and far away from Cameron.

I stumble into the bathroom, winded.

I hug the toilet, groaning. I blame the pre-drinks.

"Well, if this isn't a shitty spot for you, Jinx, the minx."

"Fuck off, Cam," I slur. Then, a wave of nausea hits me. I grab the toilet tighter, and nothing but dry heaves.

Cam chuckles. "Shouldn't have had that last drink."

I look at him, anger glimmering in his eyes. He tilts his head to one side, a smirk forming.

"I'm ready to give you some payback. My face still fuckin' hurts." His tone could shatter glass.

I knew this would come back to haunt me, but I thought he would go after Spence.

"Cam, I'll kick your ass still," I bit out each word.

I sink back against the wall, the stupidest thing I could've done. I watch as Cam approaches.

Seven

Ashton

Living with a bunch of swimming assholes is something I don't think I'll get used to. Between Ace and I talking to Prescott for the last couple of days, he still won't budge. I can't live here. Cameron, Liam, Shane, and Emery are fucking stupid. I can't stand them. They think they are the hottest things because they've been here the longest, and Cam is the captain.

Now we are setting up for a party. A back-to-school party. I didn't sign up to be an enslaved person for this house. I'm stacking solo cups out on the island when Ace walks in.

"This is fuckin' bullshit." He puffs his smoke.

"No shit, Atticus." I slam the cups down. "I heard he hosts these all the time."

He walks to the patio door, flicking his butt out. "Fuck them and their stupid pristine lawn."

"Whatever, hurry and help me. The quicker we do this, the sooner we can disappear. I'm not having anything to do with this." Rubbing at the tightness in my chest, I know what happens at these parties; that's why I can't be around them.

Ace places his hand on my shoulder, squeezing hard. "You alright?"

I clench his hand, closing my eyes. "Yep." I busy my mind with finishing this task. I can't think about that. "Are you going tonight?"

"Yeah, Mad is coming over. Get him out of that paradise he's living in."

"Ah, I see you're almost finished. Good job." Cam snaps his fingers when he walks in—nodding at my stacked cups.

I look over at Ace, whose eye is twitching. I stifle a laugh and then look back at Cam's busted face. He never did say who did it. But whoever it was, I'm sure it's because this prick had it coming.

"The party is about to start, so you are free to go. Don't forget, clean up duty tomorrow morning." He smirks.

He can take that smirk and shove it up his ass for all I care. I'll fuck up the other side of his face.

"Fuck him, captain or not. I'm not listening to him. He isn't my goddamn keeper outside of that swimming pool." Atticus sneers before walking away.

Cam better learn quickly that Atticus isn't one to follow the rules, and he never will.

———

I planned to stay in my room for the night, and you could say curiosity won. I trust a repeat won't happen because I'm not drinking tonight. I find Maddox standing between the kitchen and living room. He looks pissed.

"Who shit in your cornflakes?"

He nods to the dancefloor.

I see her dancing with a tall motherfucker. "They look friendly. Has Atticus seen yet?"

"Don't think so."

For this dude's sake, I hope not. The dip he does makes her body look fuckin' sexy. God, I've never seen her dress this sexy before. Fuck, I need to look away before I go over there and start a fight. I watch as she walks away, and her friend goes off to chat with River. The only reason I remember her name is for the rack she walks around with, and she always hangs around the house. Whoever Jinx's friend is, he's in for a world of trouble.

"You sticking around much longer?" I ask Maddox before sipping my water.

"Doubt it."

I glance at him. Something seems off with him tonight. I go back to people-watching, waiting for Jinx to reappear. I get that same sensation from a few years ago all over again. I move fast toward the direction Jinx has gone.

I grab a kid by the collar. "Have you seen a chick dressed in black, black hair?" I frantically ask.

"No, bro." I shove him back.

There are only so many rooms down this hallway; I doubt she's in the storage closet. I twist the doorknob, finding it locked. Knocking, I call out for Jinx.

"Occupied."

Cameron.

Occupied my ass, even if Jinx isn't in there. Whoever is isn't because they want to be. I jiggle the handle hard. Fuck this. I kick the handle, kicking the door in. The scene that unfolds, I see fucking red.

Jinx is huddled by the toilet, holding her high heel in the air; I can hear her wheezing. Cam doesn't seem to care. He only stands over her, ready to finish whatever he came in here to do.

"What the hell is going on?"

Cam whirled around, glaring at me. "Mind your business, Ashton. This is between her and me. Leave." He turns back to Jinx.

"Ashton." Jinx wheezes. She throws her shoe at Cam's head. He dodges it.

I make a straight line for him, grab his arm, and make him face me. "Look at me and fight, you prick. Guess I'll give you a matching cut on the other cheek."

"Fuck off,"

I'm over this. I may be a swimmer, but I grew up with a brother. One quick punch to his face, and he's knocked out. Pussy. I rush to Jinx, pulling her into my body in one fluid motion.

"Are you okay?"

"I... need my... inhaler." She wheezes.

I fiddle with her fanny pack, trying to get it unzipped.

"What the hell?" Atticus yells.

"Can't answer, busy," is all I say. I finally get it opened, grabbing her inhaler. Her shaky hands reach for it.

I watch as she takes a couple of puffs. When her body relaxes into mine, I relax a little. I brush her hair away from her face. It's been a long time since I've seen her. I watched as her green eyes became unfocused. I catch her just as her body goes limp.

"Ah, shit. Not how I wanted our reunion. I'll deal with Cam. You take her to our room." He stares down at Cam and then at Jinx.

"I got her, don't worry." I lift her into my arms, stepping over Cam.

"Ash. He didn't touch her, did he?"

"I don't think so." For Cam's sake, he better not have. Because I'll end him if he did, I push my way through the crowd, trying for the stairs. A hand lands on my shoulder, pulling me back.

"Where the fuck do you think you're taking her?" a deep voice growls near my ear.

I crank my neck, taking in the same guy that was dancing with Jinx earlier. He stands taller than I am, and I'm six feet tall. His gray eyes glare at me behind his thick black-framed glasses.

"She isn't your concern, man."

"Like fuck she isn't. Jinx wouldn't go with anyone but me."

"You can pry her from my cold, dead hands. You aren't getting her."

He stands to his full height. "She isn't an object, asshole. And if you think I don't know who you are, you are fuckin' mistaken. I've been with her for the last two years, so if you think you can weasel your way back into her life, forget it."

He leans forward, grabbing Jinx from my hands. I'm too shocked to say anything. I didn't think she would mention us to anyone, let alone a guy.

"I'll be sure to mention this when she wakes up, and she can do what she will."

I blink. What the fuck just happened? I let another guy take my girl from me. I watch as he holds her close to his chest and walks out of the house. I turn and head back to the bathroom, where I find Ace still.

He does a double take. "Is Jinx in the bedroom?"

"Not exactly." I cringe when I say it.

He stops pulling Cam's shorts down. "What?" he snaps.

"Um, her friend took her."

He raises his brow. "Friend? What friend Ash?"

"The tall motherfucker," Maddox growls.

I turn to the doorway to see him leaning against the doorframe. He clenches hard so that his scar stands out on his jaw. Cam groans, reclaiming my attention. When I see what Ace has done, I laugh.

"Oh, that's classic. Cam will rethink going after a girl again. Perfect, brother."

"I think so. Did either of you want to add to my handy work?" He holds out the razor to us.

Mad steps forward, taking the razor. He grips his dick until Cam's eyes shoot open.

"Wh-what the fuck, dude!" Cam yells.

"Don't mind me. You need a trim." Maddox grins.

Cam squirms, and I clamp my hands on his ankles while Ace restrains his arms. Cam screams as Mad does his thing. I snicker when I see what he does—leaving a nice little M in Cam's pubes.

"Guess you're Maddox's, bitch now." I release him kicking him in the ass. Wait until he sees his face for the first time. That'll be the real kicker.

"You'll regret this. You think I'll want you two living here or on the swim team? Forget it."

I shrug if I can't live here. Oh well. Good luck if Cameron thinks he can kick us off the swim team. Obviously, he hasn't figured out who our stepdaddy is yet. Besides, if he thinks the Coach will let that happen, he's fuckin' high on himself.

"Get the fuck out of here." Atticus shoves Cam, who stumbles around his shorts, which are tangled around his ankles. Maddox and I can't help but laugh.

When he finally does in the mirror, I lose it. I wipe away the tears.

"Where the hell are my eyebrows?"

"I think the better question is, how much faster can you swim now?" I snort.

Cam glares as he runs out of the bathroom.

"What a dick. Now, where the hell is Jinx?" Ace asks, looking furious that she got away.

"I would say the dorms, but I couldn't tell you which one."

Ace looks at me, blue eyes burning into my blue eyes. "We have her, yet we don't."

I feel his pain. She was so close to us, only to be taken away.

Eight

Jinx

My head doesn't feel the greatest. It's like a masonry is laying bricks on it. With a groan, I roll over.

"Morning sunshine, wanna fill me in on why I had to pull you out of some dude's arms last night?"

I swat the air. "Go away. It's too early for this."

Spence makes a buzzer sound. "Wrong, it's around noon. Now talk."

He doesn't sound happy, and for a person who's always full of pep, this makes me sit up. What the hell happened last night? And how did I end up in Spencer's bed? I stare at his anime blanket, running my finger along the stitching.

"I went to the bathroom because I felt sick. Next thing, Cam comes barging in. I tried everything I could think of, but you know, my mouth, I egged him on even more."

"Surprise, surprise. Jinx. You need to learn to shut up sometimes. Then what happened?" He sits next to me, grabbing my hand.

"I started getting an asthma attack when Ashton broke through the door. I can't remember much past that. I didn't think I had that much to drink."

Spence breathes deeply. "Cam is a fucking dead man. I knew he had something for you, but to go this far. This Ashton guy was ready to fight me over you. I'm sure he was more worried about what would happen to you."

"Or it's because you're a giant pencil."

He shrugs. "Either way. Talk some more."

I fall back onto his pillow. "Remember my stepbrothers, Atticus and Ashton." I wait for him to answer. "They also have a friend, Maddox. They start this year."

"They are the reasons you're a—"

"Say it, and I'll delete your games, asshole. No, they aren't the reasons I haven't had sex yet. You've seen the guys around campus, right?"

"I'm still not following why it matters about them."

It's a long story, one I'm not ready to retell yet. I need to stay focused now and stay away from anything boy-related.

"If you are finished with your twenty-one questions, can I go?"

He pushes his glasses up, snapping his gum. "Yeah, go. I'll see you on stream later?"

"Yeah, I'll be on." I get out of bed, looking for my shoes.

"Oh, you won't find your other one. You only came home with one."

Oh yeah, I threw one at Cam's head. I'll never see that one again. I liked those heels. Walking out of Spencer's dorm, I bump into a body.

"Sorry." I look up and freeze.

Maddox stares at me. Every muscle tensed in his body. A twitch in his jaw lets me know he's extremely pissed. Gone is the eighteen-year-old that I once knew. Now, when I look at him, all I see is pain in his eyes. He still hasn't said anything, and it's making me nervous. Without a word, he grabs my wrist and drags me to the door next to Spencer's.

"What the hell, Maddox!"

"Don't even start with me." He punches in his code, pushing the door open. With a quick shove, I trip inside.

"What was that for, ass." I glare at him as I step forward.

He crosses his arms, taking a ragged breath. I look more closely. His eyes turn distant; then he turns away.

"Things changed when you left, Jinx."

I watch as he moves to his small sitting area. He releases a large sigh as he sits. I stand there trying to figure out what the hell went on for two years that I don't know about. Why wouldn't Dad tell me what went on?

"What don't I know?" I ask cautiously. I eventually move to the couch, standing in front of him. Maddox still won't look at me. I gently reach out my fingertips and trace the edge of the scar on his jaw, and his eyes clamp shut.

"When?" I whisper.

"First year of college." He grabs my wrist. "It's something I'm not going to talk about."

"All right, are we going to talk about why you shoved me into your room? I have things to get done today."

His grip tightens more. "Who was the dick that hauled you away?"

I jerk my wrist out of his hold. "The only dick was Cam. If you mean Spencer, he's my friend, and you three leave him the hell alone. I mean it, Maddox. Don't involve him in your stupid circle jerk."

His eye twitches. "I'll do whatever I want, Jinx. If I want to drag your little bestie into my circle jerk, I will. What's stopping me?" He tilts his head.

"Why do you have to be a jerk? I'm only asking that you don't hurt him."

He huffs. "Don't worry. He's safe. He isn't who we're after."

"Do you still play the guitar?"

He nods.

"I miss playing with you, don't you?"

His eyes pierced deep, deep into mine. "No," he says through clenched teeth.

Pain grips my chest. I wasn't expecting him to be so cold toward me. I knew we wouldn't fall back to where we once were, either, but baby steps. I guess he doesn't want that. I give him a tight lip smile and back away.

"I'll see you around, Maddox. Stay out of my life, and that goes for the twins."

He doesn't try to stop me as I slam the door behind me. My emotions may have gotten the best of me back there. There's something about Maddox that gets me every time. My bare feet slam against each step as I make my way to my floor. Why am I so pissed? Pushing open the door to my floor, I'm hit with an odd sensation. Somebody has been up here recently. Perhaps a newer student is wandering around.

I need a shower; the stench has finally hit me, and I can't believe I talked to Spence and Maddox after barfing my guts out last night. Gross.

I let the warm water run down my back. I can't believe Cam would do that to me. He's on my fuckin' hit list now. That asshole had a plan the entire time. I can't be in that situation again. My only saving grace was having Ash storming in. It's been a long time since I've seen him, and fuck me. He looks so different, but he's still my stepbrother. These thoughts are not healthy. I scrub my body until my skin is pink and sore. What I need is some brainwash to remove these thoughts.

Entering my kitchen, I think about making something to eat, but the way my stomach is acting, I'm not sure I should chance it. Instead, I open my window for when Edgar makes his appearance and grab my cello. There is something powerful about playing the cello naked.

I close my eyes and play *Prokofiev Sinfonia Concertante,* letting the music drift into my bones and taking me to places I wish to go. My fingers move across the strings as images of Atticus and Ashton flash before my eyes.

I never did make good on my deal, and I'm afraid it only made Atticus want me more. It got to the point where I had to change my phone number; he wouldn't leave me alone. I was going crazy. When they said they were going to community college, I was excited. I was free of them always being around. Living with the twins was a blessing and a curse. I thought for a second that Maddox and I would be something. I just—couldn't.

Now that they are all here, my nightmare is coming true.

Maddox and Ashton probably already told him about Spencer. Now, I need to protect Spence because if I know Atticus, he'll do anything to keep me away from any guy. Even if said guy happens to be my bestie. I just wanted a stress-free year. Was that so much to ask for?

I need to avoid all three guys now. With classes starting Monday, I have no idea who is in any of them. Knowing Dad, he won't tell me. Unless.

Me: Wanna do some recon for me while I scope out the Dean's office?

Pencil: Fuck yeah, I do!

Pencil: Why?

Me: Reasons. I'll tell you when I see you.

Pencil: Meet me outside in twenty.

I throw on a pair of black leggings and a T-shirt. I look like a regular person, cringing. I tug at my shirt. If I want to blend in, I have to look like everyone else around campus. I swipe the set of keys off my counter and wait for Spence. Doing B&Es is Spencer's expertise. I guess it's not breaking in if I have the keys, but one could dream.

I slap a hand over my mouth when Spencer walks out of the Hall. He's wearing all black, from head to toe. He's even wearing a stupid balaclava.

"Spence, what the hell?"

"I'm not going down for you. I don't care how much you sweet talk your dad. I'm not losing my spot here." He walks away from me.

I run to catch up. Stupid short legs. "Seriously. I've gotten you out of so much shit, so don't even."

"Teeny, can you be a little stealthier? We are trying to commit a crime."

The sun has just gone down, and only a handful of students are milling around, and he's right. We don't need witnesses. They get a little hard to keep quiet. Sticking to the tree line, it's been our usual route since doing our late-night B&Es. If I don't have the keys, Spence will pick the lock. Nothing holds us back. The only place we don't go is the basement. During our first year attending, we heard stories about the basement, and neither of us has been brave enough to venture there to this day.

Sneaking across the path, we reach the back door without being seen. I'm still trying not to laugh at Spence—he looks so stupid. I grab my keys, unlocking the door. The one thing this school hasn't upgraded has been security, a good thing for us.

"All right, let's get this thing over with. Even though I have no idea what we are doing," Spence says when he removes his balaclava.

"I need to see what classes my stepbrothers are in."

He glares at me. "This is why I'm not at home texting big titties?"

"Yes, Pencil. Because if they are in my classes, I have time to change their schedules."

Spence grabs my shoulder. "Can't you just leave shit alone? It's too late. They already have their schedules. Your dad will know somebody fucked with the system, and who do you think he'll turn to first?"

Why does he always have to be the person of reason?

"Well, we're dressed up. What do you wanna do then?"

"Cam's car."

"Say no more, my friend."

It sucks to be Cam. He'll have a lovely surprise come morning.

Nine

Atticus

Waking up in this house is goddamn bullshit. For my plan to move out of this house, it's simple. Cam fucked up last night. Once Prescott finds out, my demands are easy. I need to watch out for Jinx and be in the same building as Ash and her.

"What the fuck happened to my car!" Cam yells through the house.

I scramble out of my bed, pulling the bedroom door open. Ash rushes out of the bathroom with a towel wrapped around his waist, his white-blond hair dripping wet from his shower.

"What the hell is happening?"

I shrug. "Beats me. From the sounds of it, someone fucked with Cameron's car."

We move downstairs to where Cameron is pacing back and forth. "Which one was it? It had to be one of you." He points to Ash and me. "You're the new fucks here. I'll give you the lowdown. No one messes with my property. That goes for my women. Fuck with me, and you'll regret it."

I chuckle, trying to take him seriously with his drawn-on eyebrows. "Yeah, no. See Cam, that's not how it works. We won't tell the dean what happened with Jinx if you leave us the fuck alone."

His face turns crimson, and he puffs his chest up. He says, "Really, why? Is that bitch yours or something?"

Ash scoffs. "Or something, and if you call her a bitch one more time, you'll see what the bottom of the pool is good for." Ash walks away, leaving Cam speechless.

"See ya around. Practice starts soon, doesn't it? You might wanna figure out your eyebrows."

If I had it my way, I would be captain.

Ash and I head over to Darrow Hall to grab Maddox. The first day of classes, and I'm already ready to call it quits before stepping inside a class. I notice Mad waiting outside, holding his guitar case. I'm glad he picked up music. It's one thing that calms him. When he doesn't play, he drinks. And that concerns me.

"Have you seen her come out yet?" Ash asks, trying to look around Maddox.

"Nothing yet, man."

I light up a smoke, wondering if we'll have any classes with her today. The unknown is what's driving me insane. I need to know. I need to see her. The fact that another man gets to see her more than me doesn't sit right.

One way or another, she will be mine.

The halls are crowded as I make my way into my psych class. I'm overwhelmed by how many people there are, and here I thought I was late. I'm so not used to this. Community College was laid back and less stressful, and the kids didn't give a shit. I find a seat in the back, over-looking everyone like peasants.

Moments later, she walks in. And my world stops. Jinx is in my class, and I can scream from the top of the world; finally, I get her to myself. I watch her scan the room, looking for a seat or friends. When her jade eyes land on mine, they snap close instantly, and her forehead creases. That's right, baby, I will make your life a living nightmare again.

I'll never forgive you for leaving me two years ago.

"Seriously, Atticus. You need to leave me alone. You can't keep texting me these things." Jinx throws her phone at me as soon as I walk into the house from swim practice. She's practically foaming at the mouth.

"Why not? I know you love it when I tell you I'm thinking about sliding my fingers inside your wet pussy, and how I'm going to make you scream my name. I can't wait to taste you on my lips, Jinx."

I move to her, pulling her ass into my growing dick. She wiggles in my arms, making me groan.

"S-stop, Atticus."

I can't help pulling her in more. I need to feel her closer. "Fuck, you feel so good next to me. You better not let anyone inside that pussy. I'll know." Licking my way up her neck, I nibble her earlobe. "I mean it, Jinx. If I find out, there will be consequences." I push her away from me.

"You're such an asshole. I can't wait to get away from you." Her black hair whips around as she spins to get away from me.

"I'll find you either way, remember. There are three of us and only one of you," I call out.

She left the following day and never came home, not even for the holidays. She simply vanished from us. We've been trying our hardest to get out of that horrible community college. That's when Ash and I set the music building on fire. They didn't like how Maddox was playing his music, and half of the asshole jerks that were in that class hated him and couldn't handle his talent. Fuck them. We lit it up like a bonfire. It got out of hand, and they automatically knew who did it. Thankfully, between Mom and Prescott, they didn't press charges. Prescott donated a hefty sum and told them we would switch schools.

Jinx slowly sits a few rows in front of me. I grab my books, moving seats.

Right.

Next.

To her.

"Morning, little grim. I'm saddened that you didn't sit by me."

Her entire body stiffens.

"Why can't you leave me alone? It's bad enough I've already bumped into Maddox and Ashton. Now you. Can't I catch a break?" She slams her book on the desk. "Jesus Christ, just once. I want things to go my way," she mumbles.

I can't help but chuckle. I lean over, getting close to Jinx.

"Never will happen. Remember what I said before you left. That pussy belongs to me, and I came to collect," I speak low into her ear.

"Piss off. I can get you kicked out of this school before you know it." She stares forward, never looking at me.

I need to see her green eyes again. Just one more time, and I'll be able to get by at least one more hour. But she never does. This class keeps dragging on, and I should be paying attention. I couldn't tell you what the professor was rambling on about, but Jinx's fingers are flying over the keys on her laptop, taking notes. I'll get them later.

When the class is dismissed, Jinx quickly throws her things in her bag and darts out of class. I lose her in the sea of students, which is difficult considering she's the only one in all black. Opening up our group chat, I send the guys a quick text.

Me: Find her. She's leaving the main building.

Ashton: On it.

Maddox: Got it.

I need to figure out her goddamn schedule. This is bullshit. This entire school is stupid. I light up a smoke as soon I exit the doors, taking an enormous drag filling my lungs. Swim practice starts tonight, and I only want my girl to cheer for me.

Ash: Found her, heading to Greywood Hall.

Maddox: That's the music hall. I have class there next.

Me: Good, it's your turn then, M. We need her, so don't fuck it up.

Maddox: Whatever man, she already came to my place.

Those two always had an easy relationship. I would be jealous over it, but Maddox needs somebody he can trust, and besides, if it weren't for Jinx, he wouldn't have found his love for music, so I can't fault her for that. She only has one fault, and I'll fix it soon.

I head to my next class, and somehow I got suckered into an art class. I swear Prescott is being a dick for a reason. I step inside and notice Ash. Thank fuck.

"You got stuck in here too?" I grab a seat next to him.

He rolls his eyes. "Don't even start. I'm stuck in some bullshit classes this term. I still don't understand why we didn't get to pick our courses."

"That's because Stepdaddy is still paying for everything. Therefore, no matter how old we are, we don't get to make up our minds."

"Yeah, well. Stepdaddy can shove it up his asshole until he can taste it," Ash growls.

The classroom doors open, and the guy hanging around Jinx walks in. My day got a whole lot brighter. I nudge Ash, nodding to where he's moving to.

"Isn't that the dude that was hanging around Jinx?" I ask.

"That's the peckerhead that stole her from my arms. I'm not doing that again."

I don't understand why Jinx chose him as someone to hang around with. Did she do it to despise us? Knowing that hanging around another guy will send us into a frenzy, newsflash, it's only to make me chase you more. Before she realizes it, I'll have her caught in my web. There won't be any escaping us. I'll tie her to my bed if I have to.

"I wonder how Mad is making out with Jinx. I didn't have much luck in psych with her."

"No text is a good text, right?" Ash shrugs.

He's the man of silence, so who the fuck knows. He'll make us wait it out until the end, anyway. It is what annoys me the most about him. But for now, I need to make a plan for the guy that's currently glaring at Ash and me.

I'll fix his problem soon, no doubt about that.

Ten

Jinx

It's the first day of classes, and I'm running on four hours of sleep. I blame Spencer, as always. Destroying Cam's car was the best, and from his lack of text messages, he hadn't figured out that it was me yet. But the big ASSAULTER I keyed on the side of his car should've given it away. The girls on campus should be aware of Cam.

I dress casually today and grab my black and white check pants and an old band tee. I do a quick double braid before finding my combat boots. I'm going to be so late for class if I don't get out of here soon. I double-check that my bag has everything I need before swiping my leather coat off my couch.

I'm halfway across the campus when I realize I should've grabbed an energy drink. Psych class is going to drain me even more.

Me: Meet me for lunch later?

Pencil: For sure, I'm going to be starving.

Me: You don't even have a morning class. Shut the fuck up.

Pencil: Tell me about it, this bed is comfy. Have fun Dickhole.

I step inside my class, and I want to die.

Atticus Banks. Of course, he would be here, and Dad would stick one of them in my classes. Why wouldn't he? I'm surprised I didn't get a phone call or text telling me to give them the royal treatment again. Why can't I just have things to myself for once? They come here like bulls in a china shop and destroy everything I've worked so hard for. I guarantee by the end of this week, all three of them will be popular, the most talked about guys here.

Considering the two are on the swim team, all the girls will be drooling over them. By the way, Atticus looks now, with tattoos peeking out from under his shirt; I can only imagine what he looks like underneath his clothes. Goddamn him.

I smell him before he even talks; my body instantly stiffens, trying to ignore him, but my pussy throbs for him. Even more, now that I haven't seen him in two years, he's changed so much, but I don't know this Atticus, and I'm not sure I want to.

I need to get the hell out of this room; he won't stop staring at me, and I can't keep my composure for much longer. Either he backs off, or I'm about to bend.

"Remember, if you miss a class, check the student portal for daily assignments. The roster is also posted for those who study faster than others. That doesn't give you bonus points. You are all dismissed."

I had never raced out of a room so fast before.

I need air.

Thank God I have music next. Nothing is more calming than playing my cello. Greywood Hall has been my favorite place on campus, and I'm not ashamed of the hours I've logged in here. Anything for that placement. I need it.

Professor Vos is already waiting for students to arrive, and my hate for him is bubbling over. All I can think about is who will be the new Piper this year. I head toward my seat and wait. I watch as Lula heads over to her Violin and winks at the professor; I guess she's my competition. How the hell am I supposed to beat that?

Lula turns her eyes on me and glares. If it's a fight she wants, I'll give it to her. She can suck that old man dick all she wants, but I'll win the old-fashioned way, with musical talent.

"Glare any harder. Your face will stay that way."

My head snaps to the side, taking in Maddox. I look down and see his guitar. "You're taking music?"

He raises a brow. "The guitar would be an indicator."

Great, now I just need to knock Ashton off my list of classmates, and my world is *complete.*

I listen to Vos give the same speech about how music is the most critical part of a person's life. Honestly, I wish he would switch it up a little. I could recap this speech in my sleep.

"This year, as most of you know, the top student will be chosen for the orchestra. You need to show up for each practice, concert, and whatever else I throw at you. You are one hundred percent commented to this."

That spot is mine.

I notice Lula inch forward in her seat. I beat her last year, only for Piper to wipe me out. I'm not letting another dick-sucking cunt steal it away again.

"Jinx, seriously, the face." Maddox hisses.

"Shut the fuck up, Maddox. You wouldn't understand."

I see him clench, making his scar protrude.

"I understand more than you would know, Jinx." He runs his finger along the scar, flinching before he drops his hand. "Some things you wish you could forget and redo, but that'll never happen. Just remember you need to live with the mistakes."

What the hell happened to him? Whatever it was, he never deserved it. Maddox was never a bad guy; he's always been gentle, even if his home life was hell. He knew what he didn't want in life, so he did the opposite of what his parents did.

I set my cello up, ready to ignore everyone, including him. But once he strums his guitar, memories threaten to seep back in. I can't let them. He shut me down earlier to play together, so he can't do it now. I need to get my head straight, or I won't be getting that spot.

Once the class is let out, I book it to the food court. I need to talk to Spence. He'll tell me what I should do. He's always talking me off the ledge, and I need to be talked down because I'm ready to jump. I juggle my cello case, trying to open my bag to get my card out. This would be easier if I had three hands.

"Teeny!" Spence yells, embracing me in a half hug, smashing my face into his chest.

I push him away and then pass him my case as I open my bag, digging my card out. "How was your art class?"

"Eh, you know how it is. Except there are two new assholes that have a hate on for me." He moves my case ahead for me.

"Cam?" I place a soup and bun on my tray. I watch Spence piles his plate full with a burger, a pizza slice, a Jell-O cup, a dessert square, plus an apple. It shouldn't surprise me by now how much he can eat, but it does.

"Actually, not Clam Jam. I'm surprised we didn't hear anything out of him yet about his car. No. It was from the Shining Twins."

Fuckin' Atticus and Ashton. We move to an empty table.

"What did they do?" I slam my tray down, spilling my soup.

He grins. "Nothing. They glared at me the entire time. If I had to guess, they wanted my dick more than anything."

I shove him. "You are not a stud, so drop it. Plus, I don't think they swing that way."

He winks. "How was music? Teach being a dick?"

I roll my eyes. I can already tell he's about to be pissed when I fill Spence in. "We have a new Piper. You know Lula Leboux?"

"Oh, Jinx. No, why doesn't this school do anything about the student-teacher relations?"

"Yeah, I saw her giving him the dovey eyes. I had to hold myself back from punching her out in class. Oh, and Maddox is in my class. All I'm missing would be the other Shining Twin, and my set will be complete."

"Gotta collect them all, right?" He chuckles.

"Like a Pokéman. Think the trade value would be worth it?" I shove a huge bite of bread into my mouth.

Spence points his pizza at me. "Honestly, they looked a little used."

I choke on my bread, coughing hard. Spence moves behind me, patting my back.

"Don't die on me. You can't leave me alone in this hellhole."

"I'm not dying. Besides, if I go, you go. I'm not doing the real hell alone," I rasp out. I crack open my water bottle, taking a huge drink—my poor throat.

"Remove your hand from her now."

I stare into a pair of ice-blue eyes across the table. Atticus' eyes burn with hate at Spencer. Ashton stands with his arms crossed, and Maddox looks bored. Spencer's hand flexes on my back, ready to grab me if he has to.

"Yeah, not gonna happen. See, my girl here doesn't fucking like you."

I try to keep a straight face, but once he says those words, Atticus' eyes twitch. World War III is about to break out, and Spencer can't fight for shit.

"The fuck she is. Who the hell do you think you are?"

Spencer moves his hand to my shoulder, and I take a deep breath. Ashton moves to Atticus' side. They may not be identical twins, but they still look like each other. The white-blond hair and ice-blue eyes are the only matching features. I look over at Maddox; his face is blank.

Why can't they just let me do my own thing?

Eleven

Jinx

The stare-down continues, and it's making a scene. I hate drawing attention to myself, especially when it happens on a daily. I touch Spence's hand.

"I'll be all right. I'll text you later, okay?" I reassure him.

"Yeah, okay." He slowly drops his hand. "If any one of you hurts her, you're fucking dead. You may think she's yours, but remember, she left you. She was only around you for a year. She's been with me longer. Who do you think she'll come to when shit hits the fan?"

He moves closer to Atticus. "News flash, it won't be you." Then he walks away.

I stay silent. Spencer has been my only friend and the only person who will stand up for me. I would honestly be lost without him. I swear he's the only one that understands me.

"Let's go someplace more private. We need to talk, Odette," Atticus demands.

Ashton grabs my cello case, and Maddox grabs my elbow, helping me up. I try to snatch my elbow back, but his hold only tightens. This is where my height sucks balls. I'm practically dragged out of the food court. We don't stop until we reach one of the outbuildings.

"Jesus, you didn't have to drag me the whole way." I brush myself off, giving Maddox the finger.

Atticus lets out a loud sigh. "Calm down, Jinx. You act like we kidnapped you."

"Ah, hello. You kinda did."

Ashton rolls his eyes. "Don't be such a drama queen. We have questions. First, who's the nerd?"

I roll my neck, and I try to keep the anger in. Then my fist flies. Landing square on Ashton's pretty fuckin' face.

"The hell, Jinx." He holds his face. "What was that for?"

"That's for calling Spencer a nerd. Only I have that right. Watch your mouth before I cut your goddamn tongue off. He's the only person I can rely on in this crappy place. Don't come around acting like you three have the right to call me yours. You never did," I snapped, anger boiling over.

All three stare at me wide-eyed.

Atticus is the first to move. His tattooed hand wraps around my neck, pushing me into the building behind me. My throat threatens to close already. Small breathes escapes, but he doesn't care.

"Listen to me and listen well. If I find another guy touching you, I will end them. You are ours. Do I need to ask the question, or shall you tell me?"

"What question." The words came with difficulty.

"Is this pussy still untouched?" He glides his other hand in between my legs, cupping my pussy. "Has anyone touched what belongs to me?"

His finger presses on my clit, his gaze never leaving mine. My fingers clawed at the building behind me as he continued to press circles, making me wet. I refuse to give him the sound he so desperately wants. It's not until he looks down and notices my nipples hardening under my shirt he laughs.

"I knew you craved this. Why fight it?"

"Because I hate you," I spat out, feeling myself vibrate with anger. Atticus' finger flexes around my neck, growing tighter. I wheeze more. My chest is on fire, trying to fight back a cough.

"Ace, I think you should stop," Ashton tells him.

Atticus finally releases me, and I bend over, coughing. A hand rubs my back carefully.

"Do you need your inhaler?" Maddox asks.

I shake my head. Luckily, it's not an attack. I straighten up, breathing deeply. I grab my case and start walking away. They don't deserve to hear anything else from me. What's the point? They won't listen to me, anyway. They haven't before; why would they start now?

If they think they control me, they have another thing coming. I dig in my bag for my phone, punching in Dad's office number. He's about to get a new asshole because I'm chewing it out. I'm done with this already, and it's only the first day. It has to be Serena's idea for them to come here.

"Hello, sweetheart. How was your first day?" His cheeriness should bring a smile, but it doesn't.

"You tell me, Dad, how do you think it went?"

It's silent for a while. "Ah, I'm not sure, but I have a feeling it didn't go well."

"Give the guy a gold star. Was it you who stuck them in my classes? I'm surprised you didn't make me give them a tour of the campus. It's the first day of school, and they are making my life a living hell. Thanks, Dad." I hang up without letting him answer. I shoot Spence a text telling him I'm locking myself in my room for the night.

With all the money this school racks in, an elevator would've been handy with renovations. But what do I know? I technically don't pay school fees. When Dad retires, this school becomes mine. He's not only the dean. He owns the fucking thing. Another secret that I hold close to my heart. Although sometimes I want to tell a few dickholes that I could ruin their lives, but I digress. It would be nice to mess with Lula and see what would happen when I tell her about her relations with a teacher.

The look on her face would set me up for life. The orchestra spot would be mine, but I would rather earn it properly. That's why I need to practice more this year. I can't let anything get in the way.

The evening is falling by the time I finish practicing. I change into a pair of black sleep shorts and a tank top. I contemplate taking my hair out, but I'm too lazy. Dad hasn't bothered calling me back. He must realize how upset I am and giving me the space I need. Not that I would answer the phone while I practice, regardless. I wouldn't stop for anything.

I do, however, find a few texts from a random phone number.

Unknown: I saw you earlier. You looked good underneath Atticus' hand. I wish it were mine instead.

I read it over and over. It has to be one of the guys playing a sick joke. Right?

I try to get it out of my head and do the small amount of dishes I have piled up. I run down to the basement and start a load of laundry. But even watching my laundry go around in circles, I can't get that text out of my head.

Who the hell was watching us? Cameron? That sick fuck, it was probably him, now that I think about it.

"Jinx."

I jump at the sound of my name. Placing my hand on my chest, I look toward the door.

"Ashton. You don't sneak up on people."

He takes a seat next to me. "I did call out to you a few times. What's got you deep in thought?"

"We aren't friends, so if you think I'm going to spill my shit to you, you're wrong. Why are you down here?"

He pulls a joint from his pocket. "I usually come down here to smoke if I'm visiting Mad, but since you're here, I won't."

I roll my eyes, hating myself a little more. "Thanks for what you did at Cam's party. I usually never get drunk at his parties for that reason. Spencer and I always stick together, but the one time I said I would be fine." I shake my head, feeling stupid.

"It's okay, Jinx. I'm glad that you have Spencer. Honestly, I do. When we weren't here to protect you, at least he was. At least you had that." He gives me a sad smile.

My heart drops. "Ashton," I whisper.

"Not today, Jinx. I'll leave you alone." He leans closer, leaving a kiss on my forehead.

I close my eyes, breathing in his fresh scent. I can almost smell the chlorine from the pool if I breathe deep enough. My eyes are still closed even after he's gone.

What happened to him? What happened to all of them? I never left broken men behind. Was I leaving them behind the thing that finally broke them? No, it can't be. They would've followed me to RWA if that were the case.

I get busy folding my laundry when a voice clears its throat.

"Can I do my laundry too?"

"It's a free country, Maddox."

Why is it the day of running into these guys? I watch from the corner of my eye as he throws a load into the washing machine. I know one thing: I find it sexy when a man does his laundry, but I also find it sexy how he stuffs the machine. Dirty thoughts are running wild in my mind.

"Nice bra." He chuckles.

I look down at my bra with spiderweb mesh and appliqué bats. "Thanks. A woman needs something beautiful on her body, don't you think?"

He slams the lid shut and turns to me. "Jinx, you could wear a brown paper bag and still be the most beautiful woman on the planet. I never understood why you care so much about what others think about you. Let the world see you be different. I would rather have you be you than a cookie-cutter Jinx. At least you aren't afraid to wear something or be something."

"You can't suddenly come here acting like we're friends."

He lifts me on top of the dryer, opening my legs wide before stepping between them. "I can do whatever I want, and you'll enjoy it."

What in the fuck? My body doesn't care, and it's giving him the green light.

I swallow hard. His hands are warm as they glide up my thighs. My breath hitches in my throat when his fingers stroke the outside of my underwear. He wraps his hand around my back, pulling me closer to his stomach.

Sliding his finger beneath my underwear, gliding through my wet folds until he circles my clit. I lean back, arching my back and pressing my pussy more into him, needing more from him.

"Maddox, please."

"Why? Why should I let you come?"

My body burns for release. Atticus started it earlier, and now with Maddox. I won't last long, and the thought that someone else could walk in here only turns me on more.

"Answer me, Jinx. Why should I let you come?"

"B-because you would be the first."

I didn't get a second to think. Maddox spreads my legs wider before sinking a finger deep inside.

"Ahh"

"Shit. You're so tight." He pulls my tank down, and his tongue flicks across my nipple, fast, wet, and quick.

My needy moans fill the room. Maddox works over to my other breast, his finger moving faster. I lift my leg onto the dryer, opening up for him, giving him more of me. He moves his lips up my neck along my jaw. When his lips captured mine, he stole my breath. Maddox kisses me like he's trying to steal my soul, burying himself deep within me. I'll never get enough of this.

"Come for me, baby. I wanna feel you squeeze my finger tight while I imagine it is my cock deep inside of you."

I grip his shoulder as a flurry of warmth washed through my stomach and spreads between my thighs, wetness gushing all over Maddox's fingers and onto the floor. I'm a panting mess when I finally come back to earth.

"God, you're gorgeous when you come. I'm glad I was the first for you." Fixing my top, he kisses my forehead and backs away.

"This doesn't mean anything." I hop off the dryer, grab my basket, and leave him behind.

I shouldn't allow myself to fall for them. But this stupid heart of mine can't seem to get the memo.

Twelve

Maddox

Jinx has always been there for me ever since the twins moved into her house. She went out of her way to make me feel welcome in her home. Not like the twins' mother; Serena's a royal bitch. Serena never wanted me around, even after she married Prescott.

She has always been a snake, and I can't stand her. No matter my family life, Serena didn't try to help. I hid it from Jinx. She didn't need to know what happened behind closed doors of the Van Daren residents. But Serena could've done something. Being an adult, she could've stopped what was happening to me. All Serena did was sit back and do nothing. She's pure evil. I was glad to be leaving that god-forsaken town to return to Jinx. She's what I need, but I feel like a pile of shit for what I did right now. I'm no better than my shitty father.

I watch Jinx walk away, leaving me alone. Always alone.

Digging my phone from my back pocket, I open our group chat.

Me: She's still a virgin.

Atticus: Good, out of all of us, she trusts you the most.

Ashton: She would trust you, Ace if you stopped being an asshole to her.

Atticus: Whatever, she'll get over it.

He's such an idiot. Jinx doesn't respond to force, and he hasn't figured that out yet.

Me: Ace, just grow a pair and give already. I'm not doing your stupid games anymore. Either you do it yourself, or I will.

That should light a fire under his ass; I don't understand why he's the one that gets to claim her first. Besides, her first orgasm will forever be mine. I'll treasure that forever. The way her pussy squeezed my fingers, I swore my dick was ready to explode in my pants. But that doesn't mean anything; I'm not good enough for her.

———

I have a hard time sleeping, nightmares plague my dreams. I move to the kitchen, opening the only cabinet with something that'll help; taking the bottle down, I move to the ugly green couch that came with the dorm. I reach for the tin on the coffee table, flipping the lid open. Weed and liquor are a person's best therapists. I light my joint, taking a few puffs, and my body sinks further into the couch. I swirl the whiskey around in the bottle before tipping it to my lips. The burn is a welcome feeling. Anything to remove those thoughts running around.

I run a finger along my scar. I was stupid that night.

Taking another toke, I try to remove those thoughts when that doesn't work. The liquor usually does the trick.

Pounding, loud pounding. Is that my head or heart?

"Wake up, sleeping beauty, school awaits."

I groan, rolling over.

"No, seriously, Maddox. It's already ten, and you missed your first class. What the fuck happened last night?"

"Ash, go away. I can't deal with you right now." I push my head deeper into the cushion, trying to relieve some pressure.

I just want to be alone. I need to figure out how to change my lock code.

"Not happening. I'm not letting you drown again. Up, let's go." He claps his hands twice, causing my head to flash with lightning bolts.

"Shut up," I groan.

"Mad, I made a promise. I'm not falling back on it. Now. Get your ass up, drink some water, and get out the fuckin' door."

Sometimes, I hate him. I roll off the couch, staring up at him. The I win written on his face tells me I'm screwed.

"I'm up."

He raises a brow. "I think you need to go back to kindergarten. You're down. But whatever. Coffee is being made. Shower, you stink."

I lift my arm, smelling my pit. Meh, it's not that bad. Ash snaps and points to the bathroom. I crawl to the bathroom, my body too sore to get up, more so my head. I flop over on my back when I get into the bathroom. The cold floor feels nice on my skin.

"I peed on the floor!" Ash yells.

Only he could ruin a good thing.

Ash and I walk out of the dorm and toward the main campus. He's smiling at everyone, and all I want to do is crawl back under my covers. I'm not in the mood for people. Ash grabs my elbow, pulling me to the side of the building.

"Here." He pulls a blunt from his pocket. "You need this more than I do."

"Thanks." I lit it up without a second thought. Becoming calm instantly. I pass it to Ash, watching him take a couple of puffs. His blue eyes shimmer in the sun. I never understood how he could go on day after day after what happened to him. I would be drowning.

He nods to the school. Do I need English studies? I doubt it; it's not like I'm looking for a career in English Lit. I'm not sure what I'm gonna do with my life. I should figure it out. I'm almost twenty-one. The only thing that I paid any attention to has been music. When Von mentioned the orchestra spot, that felt like a vision opening up. Would I be kidding myself if I thought perhaps that it could be mine?

Half the assholes in that class would be fighting for that spot. What makes me so special?

I leave Ash behind and head toward my class as I pass the office. The witch is walking out.

"Good Morning, Maddox. Staying out of trouble, I hope." Her brow raises condescendingly.

"Serena. I always stay out of trouble."

"Mmm, I'm sure."

The way her white blonde hair is pulled back into a high pony makes me want to tug it hard and punch that Botox face of hers. I don't condone violence toward women, but fuck she's the only one that I'll bend the rule for.

The clicking of her heels resonates in my brain. I should've stayed in bed.

"Mr. Van Daren, shouldn't you be someplace else?"

"I'm goin'." I don't bother looking back at Prescott—no need to see the disappointment in his eyes.

I'll always be a disappointment no matter what I do. Why do I even try anymore? I head for my stupid class. I'm sure the professor will be bitchy at me for interrupting his class. Opening the door, I take in the room. I see one seat open in the back and quickly sit down.

"Little late, don't you think?"

I give Jinx's friend the finger. "Not your problem now, is it."

"You're lucky professor dick doesn't give a shit. He places everything online and expects us to finish it at our own pace. I'm not even sure why they have him here."

I finally turn to him, watching him. What makes him so privy to Jinx's friendship? He's so normal compared to her. Is that what she needed? Someone to balance her out.

"Why her?" I ask.

His gray eyes pierce into mine. "Jinx and I are exactly alike. We are both misunderstood, we found each other, and it was like two puzzle pieces finally coming home. I can't fully explain it. She's my best friend. Should I ask why you?"

I turn away. I'm not sure why Jinx talks to me. I'm not the puzzle piece she should be looking for; she needs the corner piece that holds the entire puzzle together, and I'm not that person. I'll never be that person.

"I'm not sure why, to be honest. I didn't ask for her to befriend me."

"Well, for some reason, she did. Jinx doesn't do that for anyone. Remember that."

Now I can't concentrate. All that's going through my head now is that I have no choice but to prove to myself that I'm worthy of her. How can I do that when I can barely stand myself some days?

Leaving class, I head back to my room. That bottle is calling my name again. Halfway through, I change my mind, taking a detour to the student parking instead. It's been a while since I took my baby for a drive, and this place is already getting to me. It hasn't even been a week yet.

She purrs like a kitten when I start her up. I run my hand along the dash and feel the smoothness.

"God, I missed you." I ram it into reverse, flinging gravel everywhere. This is what I needed.

I crank the window down as I leave the gates, flipping my finger toward everyone. Maybe I won't even come back.

I keep driving until I hit the edge of Grovedale. I shouldn't go to the house, yet it calls to me. It's been four years, and it still haunts me. The house hasn't changed one bit; the shutters are still falling off the windows, the siding a faded yellow, and the deck is rotting away.

I watch the place, waiting for a goddamn miracle. Like a lightning bolt, light the place on fire. Better yet.

I climb out of the car, darting across the street. Peeking into the house, making sure it's empty. I dig into my pocket for my lighter.

The flames start slow. When I reach the car, they grow up on the side of the house. I watch until the sirens grow near.

When I reach the school, Ashton and Atticus are waiting in the parking lot, leaning against a parked car. Atticus shakes his head, while Ashton doesn't even look at me.

I'll always be a disappointment, no matter what I do.

"Care to explain where you disappeared to?" Ace asks, flicking the butt of his smoke on the ground.

I walk back to my dorm, ignoring him.

"Hey, asshole. I'm talking to you."

My arm is ripped backward, swinging me around. I push Atticus away. "Back the fuck off, Ace. I'm not in the mood."

Ace moves into my space, getting close to my face. "You really wanna start this? Then let's start it. From how you smell, I only need one guess to figure out what you were doing."

My fist clenches. My fingernails cut into my palm. Ash cuts in, pushing his brother away.

"Atticus enough," He fired off. Then he pushes me back. "And you, don't start shit you can't finish."

"You wouldn't understand, Ash. It needed to be done. Those nightmares needed to end. I can't do this any-more."

I storm off before I see the pity in their eyes. Fuck this.

Thirteen

Jinx

I've never felt so out of sorts as I did leaving that laundry room. Even days later, I can't get Maddox out of my head. The way our bodies melted together. I never knew it was possible to feel that way. I've been missing out on so much, all because of Atticus.

Opening my window for Edgar, I wait for his return. It's been a while since his last visit, and I'm getting worried. Perhaps he found another friend. I hope not. I love that feathered friend.

Gwah, Gwah.

My heart swells when I hear his call coming from a distance. I knew he still loved me. I open the window wider, hanging my head out. The school looks so tiny from way up here. I cover my eyes and peer over the tree line, waiting for him.

Gwah.

The flap of his wings grows louder, and he comes in fast. I move out of the way as he crashes on the counter.

"Edgar, what happened?" Worry gripping my chest. He can hardly hop on the table. My hands shakily reach for him. "Baby, what happened? Stop moving for a second."

I gently take him into my arms, lifting his wing, and a sob escapes. I grab a towel off the stove and wrap him in it. I'm not sure who I can ask for a ride. Spence is streaming all day, and I can't stop him in the middle of it. I rush down the stairs, banging on the door of the only other person I can trust.

"Maddox, please, I need help."

I bang louder, but nothing. Shit. I can't go to Blackwood House.

"Maddox, come on. Open up." I kick the bottom of the door, damn near shaking the whole floor.

The door flies open. "Jesus Christ, Jinx. What the fuck?" His chest heaves, his naked muscular chest.

"Jinx. What do you need that you had to annoy the fuck out of everyone?"

"I need a ride, please." I adjust Edgar. Maddox's eyes follow my movement.

"What is that?"

I rub Edgar's head. "He's my friend, and he needs help. Can you take me to the vet?" I beg him, almost pleading with him. "Please, Maddox," I whisper, "I'll do anything."

He turns and walks into his dorm, leaving me in the hall. "Well, come in. I probably should get dressed."

Why does everyone like to walk away from me? Can't they just give me an answer to my face and invite me in? I close the door behind me, taking in his living room. Empty bottles and food containers are tossed along the floor and table.

Oh, Maddox.

I lay Edgar on the couch, picking up all the bottles and garbage. When Maddox comes out, I don't say anything.

"Do you think he'll be okay? His leg, I think, is broken."

"I'm sure he'll be great. He has you, Jinx." He gives me a small smile.

Edgar has a broken leg; the vet applied a splint, and Edgar will be as good as new in four weeks. I still don't know how the little guy broke it.

"He's fine, Jinx," Maddox tells me again.

He's helping me set up an area in my dorm; this is the first time I've let anyone in my room other than Spence. Having another person here who doesn't know me feels a little strange. I can't help but watch him move around, checking everything out. Invading is what he's doing.

"I thought you came to help, not snoop."

"I am helping. I'm looking for the best spot to place him. You have a very unique space here." He moves toward my window, taking in the view. It overlooks the trees. The ones I don't dare go into.

Gwah. Edgar lets out a sad little cry. Maddox moves over to him, rubbing his head.

"Shh, little guy. It'll be okay. I'll visit every chance I get." His green eyes meet mine with a promise.

"Don't promise things you can't keep, Maddox."

Moving closer to me, he gets right in my face. "I've never broken a promise, Jinx."

His hair covers his forehead, and I can't stop myself. I brush it out of the way, getting a gentle look from him. It takes me back to when I first met him.

The summer heat is almost too much for me to take. It also doesn't help when I'm head-to-toe in black. I'm about to get up with the back gate swings open. Who are those evil little shits expecting now? I watch through my sunglasses as this little punk teenager walks through the yard wearing a leather jacket and a beanie. Even in this heat, he's dressed for trouble.

"You better give me a good reason why you're trespassing, asshole."

He stops, trying to figure out where my voice is coming from. When he finally sees me on the deck, he grins.

"I'm yours, baby."

"Nice try. Which twin are you here for, A one or A two?"

He laughs. "Is that how you tell them apart?" He walks to the steps but stops when I hold up a finger.

"No, I have other ways, but that's my secret. Promise not to tell them?"

"I always keep my promises."

"Fine, Atticus is twin A because he's shorter and lit like a fuse. And Ashton is twin B because he's sweeter and funnier. Also, he doesn't care what I do in this house."

"That makes sense. Ace has been sour since he realized he didn't grow taller than us. I won't tell him. Don't worry."

"You can cross if you must."

Apparently, he's kept his promise because Atticus never mentioned me making fun of his height, not that I have anything to say about it. But Maddox is trustworthy. I let out a sigh, resting my forehead on his.

"You've never broken anything, Maddox, and that's the problem. Maybe you shouldn't place others first for once."

His eyes fall shut, and he wraps his arms around my waist.

"Jinx, I want to tell you so much, but I'm afraid of what you would think about me after you find out, and I can't do that. I shouldn't let you near me."

"Maddox, you are not a horrible person. I won't let you believe that. But you need to stop drowning yourself in whiskey. If you need help, I'm here anytime you need me. Call me, or we can play our instruments together. I love making music together. I believe in you."

He squeezes me tighter. "Thank you for what you did earlier in my dorm. I'm embarrassed that you saw that. My life has taken a dark turn, and I'm not sure how to come back from it."

"Lean on your friends. Atticus and Ashton are there, too. Don't be embarrassed or ashamed of anything. We will always be here for you. Don't fight your demons alone."

We sit silently for a while; the only sounds are from Edgar sleeping in his new home. My phone dings, breaking the silence. I don't want to leave Maddox's embrace; it feels lovely.

"Do you need to check that?"

"It's probably Spence. No one else writes me."

He hums. "I had a conversation with him. He seems like a decent guy. He cares a lot for you."

"He is. He's my best friend." I move to grab my phone. Opening the message.

Unknown: Great view the other day. I could make you come too, but with my tongue.

An image of Maddox and me in the laundry room is attached. I drop my phone, my body shaking.

"Jinx, what's wrong?"

I back away from my phone like it's on fire.

"You need to leave. Now."

He stands, grabbing my arm. "What the hell happened? You're pale. Who just texted you?"

"It's none of your business. Get out," I demand.

When he doesn't move, I yell at him again, "Get out, Maddox."

Dropping my arm, he moves to the door, shaking his head. "Remember, you wanted to help me. I'm here if you need me. But only if you want the help, Jinx."

The door closing is my undoing. I drop to the floor, reaching for my phone. Who the hell is sending me these messages?

Me: Who the hell is this?

I'm tired of it. If this is Cam, I'm going to kill him.

Unknown: Oh, you know who I am, but good luck figuring it out. You'll never see me coming.

Me: If this is Cam, I'm not playing anymore. Stop this.

Unknown: This isn't Cameron.

If it's not Cam, then who the hell is it? One of his minions from the swim team? I don't socialize with anyone else around school.

All I know for sure is they caught me twice with the guys. I can't let it happen anymore. I can't be seen with them. Distancing myself is clearly what's best. But why the sudden interest in me? I've been at the school for going on three years, and no one besides Cam has tried anything. That's why I believe it's either Liam, Shane, or Emery.

Now I need to figure out who.

Fourteen

Jinx

Mondays are the worst. Murphy's Law is true. First, my alarm never went off, making me late for psych class. So late that I interrupted class. Second, my cello string broke, throwing off the entire orchestra. I never wanted to crawl under a rock more than the second Lula turned and chuckled. I always check my strings the night before.

On top of that, Edgar was squawking all night. Poor guy must be in so much pain. I'm hoping he starts to get better soon; he was resting when I left this morning. I should check on him. That gives me a good excuse to ditch Spencer. I haven't been hanging around Spencer. I'm sure he's getting worried. We never spent a single day not talking or seeing each other. My mind hasn't been the same since getting the last text from *Unknown*.

I sneak away, heading back to my room before my last class. I'm sure Edgar is fine, but I need to make sure. Is this how mothers are? It's only ever been Dad and me, and I didn't get the nickname Jinx for nothing. I'm literally bad luck. My mother died from complications during childbirth. I never asked Dad the reasons; I assumed it was a hemorrhage.

My phone dings from inside my fanny pack. My guess is it's Spence. Cue the worst friend ever. I fish it out, opening the messaging app.

Dad: Call me when you can.

Well, that's not what I was expecting. Usually, Dad never sends me a text. When Dad sends a warning text, the call can't be good. Why else would somebody send a text telling them to call? It's usually never good news.

Kraa.

"Awe, baby. Did I wake you?" Edgar shakes his head from his bed when I close the door behind me. "I didn't mean to. How are you feeling?"

He tries to hobble over to the edge of his bed, but I stop him.

"Not so fast. Doc said you need rest. Want a treat?"

His head turns from side to side. *Gwah.*

I dial Dad on my way to Edgar's treat container. I might as well get this over with. Fishing two treats out, I wait for

Dad to answer his phone. When his voicemail kicks in, I hang up and call the office phone. Edgar shakes his body when he sees his treat as I near.

"Hello, you reached Dean Hawthorne. How can I help you?" Florence answers.

"Hi. Florence, it's Odette—"

"Oh, yes, I'll transfer you now."

She's very efficient, I'll give her that. I watch Edgar chow down while I wait for Dad to answer.

"Odette, sweetheart, how are you?" His easy-going personality is coming out.

His voice always brings out a smile. "I'm perfect, Dad. How's dealing with all the newbies?"

His deep sigh says it all. "You know how it is. Change this, change that. I don't like this room. My roommates are horrible. It never gets old, pumpkin. But I wouldn't change it for anything. Now, tell me, how is music going? Is Von being a? What are the kids saying these days? Cuntfucker."

"Dad! What the hell? Who says that?"

"What. Von is, and you can't say he isn't. I can't stand that guy."

I can't believe he dropped the cunt word. Never in my life did I think, out of all people, my dad would say that.

"Yes, well. I'm going to get that spot this year. I worked my ass off last year and lost for reasons. But not this year. I'm getting it. It's my only chance to get to my goal."

"Honestly, if I could fire him, I would. Unfortunately, he's the only one who teaches at that level. You know, if they knew you kinda owned this place, it would help a little more."

"No. I don't want that. I want to win from talent alone and not from my name. We agreed to this."

"I know what we agreed on. That was before. Anyway. I'm sorry about your brothers."

I laugh. "Don't act like you didn't stick those weasels in my classes. I'm surprised they aren't all living in the dorms."

He bursts into a nervous laughter. "Those two tried so hard to move in with Maddox. I know what Maddox needs, and it's not living with those two. I have a room coming available soon, though, and I'm sure they'll want to move into it."

Excellent, my worst nightmare is coming true.

"I should let you go, Dad. I'm gonna be late for my next class."

"All right, sweetheart. If you need anything, you know where I'm at. Love you."

"Love you too." Hanging up, tapping the cell on my forehead. I'll never get away from those guys. I'm just glad no one can move up here with me.

I'm not sure why I signed up for Business Management. It was the worst decision at the time of choosing courses, oh well. Maybe if I ever open my own school, this will be useful. This class is going to kick my ass; I barely made it through the last class.

I've just set my laptop down when a body sits beside me. It's like déjà vu all over again. The fresh scent floats over to me in waves. Ashton.

"I didn't know you were in this class?"

"I wasn't. Supposedly, Coach says I need to improve my grades and thinks this would be the best class. Bullshit if you ask me. Not sure what I need a business class for."

Ashton has always kind of been a mystery to me. He doesn't open up around me; he's more reserved compared to Atticus. Having said that, he's still a major asshole. I've seen both sides of him.

He shifts slightly in his seat, facing me. "Tell me, Jinx. Why are you in this class?"

"Stupidity, really." I shrug.

"Well, aren't we just a pair? Think we can make it through this?" He stares at the front of the class, shaking his head when the professor chats about accounting. "We are so fucked, baby."

He might be. I like math.

Halfway through class, Ashton groans. Disturbing my flow. "What now?"

He rests his head on my shoulder. "I can't compute all these numbers."

I shake my shoulder, making him sit up. "Sucks to suck, asshole. Should've paid more attention in school instead of chasing all those girls."

"I have no clue what you're talking about. I was a good boy. Ask my mother." He smirks.

He knows how I feel about his evil mother. I knew something was off with her when she started dating my dad. No one produces twins that are like these two. They don't even mention their dad; how crazy is that? I never had the nerve to ask where he was. I'll bet he ran from the witch. If she ended up dead today, I wouldn't cry or attend the funeral.

"Good boy, is that what we're calling you? I have other words."

His eyes light up. "Yeah, like what? Incredible, jaw-dropping."

"No. Donkey, douchebag, oh, and Dad's new favorite word. Cuntfucker."

His jaw drops. "Wow. Okay. No, stroking the ego, I see. That's fine. I'll do some stroking when I get back to my room."

I shove him. "Gross."

"Unless you wanna do it for me?" He runs his fingers along my jaw, licking his lips.

Goosebumps perforated down my nape, and he wagged his eyebrows at me. My gaze drops all the way down. *And* he's hard.

"Excuse me, Miss. But I do believe my eyes are up top."

I snap my gaze back up, meeting his blue eyes.

"We can always leave class if you want. See how many sounds I can get out of you while you suck my cock. I wanna watch while it disappears completely into your mouth, while tears leak out of your eyes as you gag on it."

The inside of my thighs are now wet; squeezing them together to relieve some pressure, I turn back to the front to refocus.

"What's the matter?" He whispered into my ear, his breath hot against my skin.

Grateful for the class to be dismissed before I had to answer. I shove everything back into my bag and make my escape. I don't make it far before Spencer finds me.

"The fuck, Odette. Ignoring me now?" He snaps his gum at me.

"It's not like that." I'm being shoved around in the hall, stumbling into Spence.

He grabs me, hauling me down an empty hall. "It seems like you've been acting differently since your asshole brothers arrived."

A little white lie can't hurt, right? "I've been ditching you for my bird."

He blinks. "Is that code word for something?"

I roll my eyes. "No, dickhole. Edgar had an accident, so I headed to my room to check on him. Did you survive eating lunch alone?"

He shrugs, pushing his glasses up. "Yeah, you know. Wasn't a big deal." He toys with his fingers.

"Okay, hotshot. Walk it off. We can have supper together if that makes you feel better."

He wraps his arm around my shoulder, steering me out of the school. I catch Ashton walking out, shooting Spence a glare.

Fifteen

Atticus

The smell of chlorine reminds me why I'm here. Who would have thought being forced into swimming would be the only thing I love about this school. I only wish our captain wasn't such a shit. Cam eyes me the entire way to the benches. He's been a thorn in my side since the first practice. It doesn't help when he has his buddies always backing him up, either.

He's such a pussy.

I take in the bleachers, trying to see who all showed up. Why people enjoy watching us swim is mind-boggling. Almost every seat is filled. You can't honestly tell me there isn't anything better to do around this school. Why they couldn't start a football or basketball team is weird. Then again, most of the students here are pretty prissy.

Then my eyes land on her. My girl finally showed up to watch me. I take her in, her hair down, covering most of her face. She has oversized sunglasses on, and she's wearing a big bulky jacket. If she's trying to hide from me, it's not working. I'd find her anywhere.

Ash also sees her and grins. He keeps his feelings for her close and hasn't spoken much about her, but I can tell he wants her. It's only a matter of when before Ashton makes his move. I need to make her mine first because if he takes her first, I'll never forgive him. She's mine, first and foremost.

Coach blows his whistle, giving us our ten-minute warning. I watch Cam, Emery, Liam, and Shane joke around. We don't have an extensive swim team, but I would have assumed more would've signed up for the only sports team on campus.

Ash and I are outsiders, and they try to out swim us every time we get in that water. They forget that we are supposed to be working together. It doesn't matter who can swim the fastest. *Ash, by the way.* It's about kicking Grovedale's ass come nationals. At this rate, Cam isn't going to be making it there. I'll be kicking his ass.

I make sure to face Jinx as I lower my pants. It's been a long time since she's seen my body. If she thought my tattoos ended on my arms and neck, she was wrong. I'm covered in them; I even added a little surprise someplace else for her. I'm sure she'll appreciate it when she sees it for the first time. I watch her hand lower her sunglasses, and her green eyes meet mine. I nod in agreement.

All for you. I mouth out. I unzip my hoodie, showing Jinx my chest. It's all worth it; I know she's into it. No one squirms in their seat that much. I've constantly been thinking of what Maddox confirmed. That she's still a virgin. I need to taste that pussy. I want to feel it strangle my dick and milk me dry.

"In the water, boys. Warm up, and then we'll start with 100-meter races," Coach yells before blowing his whistle.

Good thing, too, because I'm starting to grow a stiffy.

My muscles are screaming at me by the time I touch the wall. It's only two laps, and we still have a 400-meter race. If the coach tells me to quit smoking, you bet your ass I'll tell him to shove this team up his pisshole.

"You're slacking, Ace."

"Something like that. My mind is elsewhere." I push myself out of the pool, reaching for my towel.

He slips his goggles off and laughs. "I see her, Ace. Just seal the deal already. You're torturing yourself daily, being here."

"Well, I don't see you doing anything," I snap.

Ash simply shrugs. "She'll come to me when she can't stand it any longer. Don't you worry, your little black heart, brother."

Cocksucker, he needs to open up to her first. I doubt he will, though. I leave him be for now. I need to talk to coach about electing a new captain.

"I heard she gives amazing head. Next time, I'm gonna give that mouth a try," snickers Emery.

"No, I heard it was anal. That it was tight," Liam confirms.

I walk past them, sick fucks. At least when I talk shit about a woman, it's usually to her face or to the back of her head while I'm pounding into her.

"Are we talking about Jinx?" Cam asks.

My feet halt, and I turn around and move back.

"What the fuck did you just say?"

Cam crosses his arms and smirks. "Oh, I was telling the guys about Jinx. She came to my room the other night and didn't get much sleep if you can imagine."

I nod, raising my brows. "You don't say. How tight was that pussy of hers?"

Cam curls his finger into his thumb tightly together in an O shape. "So tight, I saw stars, man."

My fingers curl into a fist. "I bet." I grit out. I throw my fist into his face, sending him stumbling to the ground. I straddle him, sending punch after punch into his face.

"If I ever hear you talk about Jinx again, a messed up face will be the last of your worries. Maybe choose another person to have your sick sex fantasies about."

"Atticus, locker room now!" Coach yells.

Ash pulls me off, but not before I get one last kick into his ribs.

"The fuck. Wanna explain?"

"No." I storm off to the locker room, punching the mirror at the entrance. "Fuck!"

Whatever is in my path is destroyed. My ears ring as rage storms through my body. How long has Cam been spreading shit about Jinx? She's been here without us for the last two years if he's been pulling this shit for that long. I punch the nearest locker.

"Goddamn it," I scream, blood dripping from my knuckles onto the tile floor.

"You about finished?"

Resting my forehead on the locker, I ignore the coach.

"Very well then. I would hate to suspend you from the team. You're one of the best swimmers we have, Atticus. I can't have teammates fighting each other. For now, get dressed and take a seat on the bench. You can chat with the dean tomorrow. Is that clear?"

"Yes, sir."

Once he's gone, I sink to the floor, banging my head on the locker. I swear, next time, Cam will be a dead man. A gentle knock pulls me out of my thoughts.

"Atticus?" her gentle voice calls out.

The last person I want to see. "Not now, Jinx."

Glass crunching under her steps tells me otherwise. I should know better. She never did listen to me.

"What the hell was that out there? I know Cameron can be the world's biggest pinhead, but seriously that." She points over her shoulder. "In front of children, Atticus. Come on."

I stand, pinning her to the lockers. "That, pinhead," I growl. "Was saying shit about you. Do you know what Cameron says about you behind your back?"

She looks down and gives a clipped nod. I smack the locker, making her whimper.

"The fuck, Jinx. You let him get away with that shit?"

She shoves me back. "What the hell do you expect me to do? He hasn't learned yet that I don't want him. I've tried everything, but nothing works, Atticus. Spencer even tried fake dating me for a while, and even that was a bust. The guy is deranged."

I take a couple of deep breaths before I go back out there and literally kill that prick. I grab my bag from my locker, distracting myself.

"Anything else I should know, Jinx?" I pull on my jeans, glaring at her.

Her eyes shifted to the left before meeting mine. "No, that's everything."

Liar.

"You should go then. Want me to text Mad so he can walk you back to your dorm?"

"I have his number. I can text him. He wants to visit Edgar."

I raise my brows. "Who?"

If she has another guy, I can't deal with this again.

"Edgar, he's a raven. He was hurt, and Maddox helped me with him."

"A raven? Like as a bird? Are you feeling okay? Should I start calling you Cinderella?"

She chuckles. "Well, I do have an evil stepmother and two stepbrothers." She shrugs.

I move in again. Pinning her to the locker once more. "Yeah, but in this story, there is no prince that's going to save you now, is there?" I tip her chin upward, lips closing in on hers. She tastes like sin and paradise, and I want more.

Pulling her closer, I savor each moan that slips from her lips. Those will be mine forever. Her hands work into my hair, tugging it back until we lose connection.

"Fuck me," she pants.

"I'm down anytime."

"Never. Just because you think you have a claim on me, it won't happen."

I wrap my hand around her throat. "It will happen. You will do it, and you will enjoy it."

Her eyes widen and then narrow. "Fuck you." Rearing her head back, she spits in my face.

I back away, giving her a deep chuckle as I wipe my cheek. "Oh, little grim." A cynical smile twisted my lips. "You won't see me coming now. You better pray I never catch you when I do."

I point to the exit, turning my back on her.

Sixteen

Jinx

Fuck you, Atticus stupid Banks.

Since when do I take orders from him? I would never have thought he would lose his ever-loving mind during a swim practice in front of families. I get Cam can be a major douche but save it for some place private, like behind the building. Oh, when I get my hands on Cam, I'll make it clear again. I thought it was working, he hadn't tried talking to me since his party. I guess sometimes quiet isn't always a good thing.

Cam has officially moved to number one on my suspect list. I had one reason for going to the swim practice: to search his locker. But the asshole fucked that up. Now,

I have no choice, and I have to do the one thing I swore I wouldn't do again.

It must be someone in Blackwood House.

Me: When's the next party at Clam Jams?

Pencil: Oh, if it isn't the stranger.

Me: Shut it. Do you know or don't?

Pencil: I might. Why? Are you finally gonna get rid of that v-card?

He probably has a pool going on for the day I finally have sex.

Me: Spencer Aaron Coldwell. Answer the question, or the streams go live across campus.

Pencil: Meanie! He's having one this weekend. You really wanna go?

Me: I have a mission. You in?

Pencil: Sure. I need some spice in my life.

Perfect. My weekend is planned. Too bad it's only Wednesday. Why is this week dragging? I need more excitement in my life. I know I could tell Maddox to come by and see Edgar, but I'd rather be alone tonight. My snack cupboard is yelling my name, yes, a big bowl of popcorn drowning in butter. Oh, my mouth waters just thinking about it.

I climb the remainder flights of stairs, heading to my room, dreaming of curling up in bed with a good horror movie. That is until I see a body resting against my door.

"Atticus called."

"Obviously, he just can't stay out of shit, can he?" I brush past Maddox, opening my door.

He places his hand on the doorframe, halting my move.

"He told me what Cam said. You okay?"

I close my eyes, dragging in a lung full of air. "Maddox, I'm used to Cameron's ways. The first time he tried anything was the last party I went to. Before that, it never went that far. It's always been him trying everything to get into my pants. He's a perv that wants the weird chick, that's all."

"I don't believe that, Jinx." His eyes narrow as he searches my face.

I duck under his arm so he can't see the worry taking over. "Yeah, well, that's how it is. Come see Edgar."

Surprisingly for a bird, he's healing fast. I'm not sure what it is about this raven. Nevertheless, he's meant to be in my life.

I watch Maddox get on his knees and gently rub Edgar's head with his gentle coos; he relaxes Edgar and me. I move around the kitchen, gathering my popcorn and butter. I'm still watching my movie; my date with a certain masked man can't wait.

"Did you wanna stay and watch a movie with me?" I hold up my DVD and wiggle my brows.

"I see nothing has changed. Still not the romantic, are you."

I stick my tongue out. "Romance sucks. Are you watching this with me or not?"

He snatches the movie from my hands; I guess I'll grab the popcorn. I find him lying on my bed, hands behind his head, comfy as ever. He pats the spot next to him.

"I don't bite." He grabs my popcorn, placing it on the end table.

I climb into bed, lying next to him. I'm not sure what else to do. My lack of experience surely shows. I hear him sigh, his arm wraps around me, and the world spins. I look up into his hazel eyes.

"You can't watch a movie if you're stiff like a board, Jinx. Relax, it's only me."

Grabbing my thigh, he wraps it around his waist. My skirt falls against my stomach, showing off my black thong.

"You are quite the distraction, Jinx."

Screams from the movie play in the background. The only screams I hear are mine in my head when he runs his finger along the outside of my thong. Screaming at him to touch me where I need him the most; I need to feel his fingers deep inside me again, flexing my hips to drive home the point.

"Maddox, please."

"Nah, not tonight. You owe me something." He moves away from me, unbuttoning his jeans. I watch his hand dip in and pull his dick out.

Maddox takes my hand, sitting me up, and I square my shoulders. I can figure this out. How hard can it be? Do I lick it like an ice cream cone? Or a lollipop?

"Don't overthink it here." He stands. "Move closer, open wide, stick your tongue out, watch the teeth. I'm not into that."

I do as I'm told. Opening wide, a low sound came deep from his chest. He rakes his hand through my hair, gripping it tight.

"Remember, this is more for me than you. Make me come, baby girl."

I watch as he strokes himself, then smacks my cheek with his dick. I look through my lashes, and his mouth lifts with a wicked smile. He slides his dick inside my waiting mouth, stretching my lips to accommodate his wide dick.

"Jinx, your mouth feels like heaven."

He thrust his hips driving his dick further back. I swallow, and his grip tightens in my hair.

"Oh holy, fuuuck." He groans.

He picks up the pace. I didn't think this would be such a turn-on for me. I spread my legs, slipping my finger under my thong, circling my clit. I moan around his dick, drooling down my chin.

"I wanna feel that wet pussy on my cock, baby. Lay down."

Maddox pulls out, pushing me back. His fingers slip under my thong, slipping them off.

"I can't have sex with you, Maddox."

He flips my skirt up, pushing my legs wide. "Shh, don't worry about that." Stroking himself, his hand brushing against my clit. "I'm gonna come all over this pretty pussy."

"Please, I wanna feel your dick on me." I raise my hips, getting impatient.

A groan slips past his lips as he starts thrusting against me. My legs fall wider the faster he goes, and energy zips through my body. Our heavy breathing pickups and moans outperform the sounds from the TV.

I cry out his name when warm ropes of cum spill all over my pussy.

His thumb caresses the inside of my thigh, staring at his handy work. Swiping his thumb through his cum, pressing hard on my clit I grip my blanket.

"I think I lied. Maybe this night is also about you. Give me one more, Jinx."

"Ahh." My leg shakes as more pressure builds. "Oh, shit."

His large hand grabs my breast, pinching my nipple hard, and then I explode.

"Beautiful, baby." He fixes my skirt. "Now, if you don't mind, I would like to watch the movie." He flops next to me.

I burst into laughter. "You don't even like slasher films."

"No, but you do."

I think I just died. This man can say things to me but can't say nice things about himself.

The only thing I want more is for him to love himself. I want to ask so many questions, but I don't want to ruin what we have going on. I curl into him.

I trace his scar. I press a kiss and whisper, "I hope whoever did this got it worse."

"Don't worry. Your brothers took care of it. They may be assholes, but they do take care of those that they love. No matter what you think, their love runs thick through their veins. Surprising, considering who their mother is."

I snort. "Sorry. I hate that woman."

"Same, baby. For reasons."

I furrow my brows. "Like what?"

"Not tonight, movie."

And he's officially shut down. I go back to watching Michael Myers slice and dice some babysitters and dream of happier times for Maddox.

It's not much longer before he falls asleep. "I would do anything to take your demons away." I slip out of bed, making my way to the bathroom to change into pajamas.

Not feeling overly tired, I make my way into the living room. Edgar pokes his head up before settling in. My baby sits in the corner, waiting for me. I need to get my ass in gear and practice more. My piece is complicated. With one slip-up, you'll be able to tell.

Some say the cello sounds sad. They could be right. When you play *The Sound of Silence,* it's somber. But sweet Jesus, it's relaxing; my mind has never been more open than when I play. Hitting the chorus, my eyes close, and my body sways.

All I want is for Maddox to be free from his demons and for Ashton to find freedom from what's hurting him. And Atticus, lord, I don't think there's enough in this world to help him. He needs so much help that I'm afraid that if I slip up, or even if his brother did, that would be the end of him.

A hand lands on my shoulder, causing my bow to skip along the strings. When I look up, Maddox caresses my cheek.

"Come back to bed, baby. You play beautifully, but I need you next to me now."

"Since you asked so nicely."

He helps me place my cello in the case. Then stands there staring at it.

"You know, I never did ask why a cello even when I first heard you play."

I run my hand along the case. "It's kinda funny, I suppose. I wanted to play double bass; it was the largest string instrument, and I wanted it. I don't have to say it, but my height caused an issue, so I settled for the cello. Best choice I've ever made."

He smiles. "I can tell you pour your entire soul into it when you play."

"I need to. That orchestra spot is mine this year. Lula can suck Von off somewhere else. That's not going to ruin my chances again."

"Excuse me?"

"Last year, Piper and Von were an item. I did everything that was asked, and I still didn't get the spot. Piper must've had a golden vagina because he gave it to her, so now she's living the life in New York. I could've been out of here already."

A look passes over his face. It's gone before I can figure it out.

I grab his hand, hauling him back to bed.

One dream at a time.

Seventeen

Jinx

"Oooodette," Spencer calls as he enters my dorm.

I need to change my door code. It's like having that annoying younger brother who never knocks.

"Spencer," I mumble. I stuff another Oreo in my mouth and go back to my movie.

"Ah, the party. Aren't we going?" He snatches a cookie from the tray, getting crumbs all over my blanket.

I want to change my mind and not go; I rather stay in and eat all the cookies in the world. Then again, I'll never find out who *Unknown* is. I hate when he does this to me.

"Fine, but I'm not dressing up, and I'm not drinking."

"Dress up, and it's a deal."

"Dress up, and it's a deal," I mock. "Shut that cakehole, and it's a deal." I watch as he shoves another Oreo in and grins. I reluctantly roll out of bed to change. I'm about to enter the bathroom when Spencer yells at me.

"Something hot and sexy! I wanna see that ass bounce on the dance floor."

He's lucky he's my best friend.

———

"I still can't believe you chose this outfit. It's not hot or sexy, Teeny."

I look down at my black jeans and hoodie. It's practical for my recon, and this way, I'll blend in with the regular people. It should be easier to sneak away without getting caught.

"It's needed. Remember why we're going to this party, Spence. It's not for tits and ass."

"Just a little ass?" He holds his finger and thumb inches apart.

I smack his shoulder. "Maybe after."

As always, the front of the house is already littered. It seems worse this time around; more bodies spill around the property, and the front door is wide open with people coming and going. Loud cheers are heard from deep within. My heart skips a beat when I think about Cam and the bathroom. I was stupid and shouldn't have let my guard down. I won't ever let myself do that again.

Spencer leads the way like always, and our fingers are interlocked the entire time to the kitchen. The music thumps through my chest, almost leaving me winded.

"Drink?" Spence yells.

"Water this time."

Clear head, that's what I need. Nothing is getting in my way.

Then my eyes lock with them. Two pairs of blue and a set of hazel. A minor hiccup and a serious problem. I need to avoid them like the plague. I watch them as I drink my water, laughing inside at the eye twitch from Atticus. I won't be able to hold him off for much longer, and it scares me.

"The dance floor, Teeny." Spence sways backward. I follow; he is doing me a favor.

The song switches to *Only Girl in the World,* and I'll admit my inner romantic emerges. Who doesn't want to be the only one in a guy's life? To be worshipped and protected. I stare at all three, waiting for them to make a move.

Ashton moves first. He's wearing jeans with rips at the knees and a white tee. A crooked smile tugs at his lips.

"Well, if it isn't my favorite little melanophile."

I give him a tight lip smile. "Funny."

Wrapping his arm around my waist, he brings me in close. The muscles of his abs flex under my hand; one thing is sure. Swimming has done him good. He wraps his other hand around the back of my neck, pulling my head back. His lips brush against my throat, sending tingles down my spine. The worst thing about Ashton is that he has a way of sending me into a frenzy and then walking away.

"I can't wait to have this body. I'm going to mark you as mine." He releases me and then walks away. Leaving me breathless and horny.

A new mission, find his room and dry hump his pillow. I watch as all three of them turn and leave for the kitchen. All that's left is to locate Clam Jam and his crew. Also, where the fuck did Spencer go?

What's the point of having a number two if he can't stick close by? Where the fuck is River? Wherever her tits are, he's nearby. Whatever, I don't need him. I sneak out the front door, walking around the side of the house. Those dickwads gotta be out back; they never miss one of their parties. If they did, why host one?

The backyard is busy, just like inside. Half of these students I've never seen before. How do they know this is the hotspot already? I scan the crowd for Cameron. When I see his perfectly styled coffee-brown hair, I want to vomit. He slowly turns his face to talk to Emery—I chuckle. The right side of his face is bruised and swollen still from Atticus.

Prick.

With all the guys accounted for, I head back inside. It's time to start this. I need answers, and I want them now. I take the stairs two at a time to the first floor. I'm not even sure whose room is whose. The swim team isn't that large, but there are four floors to cover.

I push open the first door, walking in on someone in the middle of pound town. The next couple of bedrooms are busts onto the second floor. I open the first door and get a whiff of Liam's cologne. Jackpot.

This room is a disaster. Clothes are spread every-where; thank God I'm wearing my combat boots. The only furniture here is his bed, desk, and a nightstand. I guess he doesn't believe in reading. His desk isn't much cleaner, and papers are half hazardously spread. The drawers come up empty. I cross over to the nightstand and cringe as I pull open the drawer and see boxes of condoms. *Easy there, Casanova.*

Leaving empty-handed, I cross the hall to the next room. Fingers crossed, it's Emery's room.

I'm pretty sure that was Emery's room, but it was oc-cupied. I have yet to find Atticus' or Ashton's room. If they were smart, they locked their doors. One more room on this floor, and I'm already losing hope.

The room at the end is lucky number—what would it be since two were bangers? I enter the space, and it's filled with swimming trophies and medals hanging on the walls.

Cameron's room. Jackpot baby.

His bookshelf is the first place I look, and I pull books out, searching behind all the hardbacks. I'm surprised that Cam has books, to be honest. He doesn't come across as the type that knows how to read. I find a box hidden behind a stack of books, and my nerves are on fire as I open it; when I see nothing, I slump against the shelf—looking over to his desk. I crawl quickly, ripping open every draw, shuffling through whatever he has in here—still nothing.

Where else would someone hide something? I remember when I tried to hide my diary from Dad. I crawl to the bed, lifting the mattress; my heart pounds loudly, only to burst seconds later.

"The fuck." Dropping my head, I want to cry. I was confident it was him. I hear giggles in the hallway right before the door handle jiggles. Oh shit.

I dash for the closet, and sweat glistens on the back of my neck when Cameron enters the room with a very giggly girl. Oh, please tell me I don't have to witness this.

"On your knees, Juliet."

Yep, I guess I am. I screw my eyes closed tight and clamp my hands over my ears. I'm not going to listen to Juliet giving him a blowjob.

Even with covering my ears, I can hear the slobbering mess going on out there. Juliet's annoying moans tempt me to blow my cover to escape this torture. I can't even explain, Cam. That dirty talk, or whatever he's trying to do, is gross. It's quiet for a little while, and I drop my hands.

"Thanks, Doll. See yourself out."

No. You need to leave, too. Ah, shit. How the hell am I going to get out of this? I wait, but all he does is walk around his room. He touches his desk before swinging his head to the bookshelf. *Oh shit.* Does he know that I've been digging through his stuff?

Cam reaches for a box on the top, hidden behind some trophies. I swear if he pulls out a cell phone, I'm bursting through this door. He pops the lid off, and I'm on edge waiting. His hand emerges holding something, I can't tell what it is, and I'm getting impatient. I shift my foot, bumping into an object.

I hold my breath as Cam's head snaps in my direction. He steps in my direction when a pound on his door steals his attention.

"Yeah, what is it?"

I release my breath, thanking whatever God there is. The music grows loud when he opens his door.

"Someone was in my room."

"Emery, everyone is fucking. Maybe lock it next time." His voice grows quieter when he closes the door.

Me: Where the hell are you?!

That dick owes me.

Pencil: Calm down. I'm still down here, looking for you.

Me: That's great and all, but I'm stuck in Cam's room. Recon mission remember?

Pencil: Right. I'm coming.

I still need to know what Cam took. If it was the phone, how the hell could I go to get near him without me getting close to him?

A rap on the door pulls me out of my thoughts. "Psst, it's me. The coast is clear."

I yank the door open and glare up at Spence. "You dickhole. You left me alone. You know what I had to listen to in there." I shiver at the memory. "It'll haunt me until I die, and then I'm coming back to haunt you."

"It couldn't have been that bad, Teeny."

"Cam, Juliet, and a blowjob."

His face scrunches up.

"Yeah, buddy. Get me the hell out of here. I might need that drink after all."

Starting Monday, a new Jinx will emerge. No more Miss nice girl. This bullshit ends now.

Eighteen

Atticus

I want to admit that the weekend went wonderfully, but that would be a downright lie. Mother insisted that Ash and I come home yesterday for a family dinner. I'm confused as to why she would call it a family dinner when Jinx is never there. Mother could never let her anger go, I'm not sure what the hell happened, but from day one, she never did like Jinx. I can't say much—I didn't either. She's slowly growing on me.

The only good thing that came out of dinner was Prescott telling Ash and me that a room was available in Darrow Hall. I've never wanted to jump for joy before, but I came close. It's still not large enough for Maddox, but he does like to be alone.

First thing after classes, I'm moving. I'm not even waiting for Ash—one-for-one, we ain't the musketeers.

It's been a hot minute since I've been to this stupid art class. I'm not one to paint portraits of apples in a bowl. Perhaps two apples and a banana, but I feel the teacher wouldn't appreciate my artistic view. Ash was the one that developed that bone; that prick can paint anything, and it'll look decent. I'll assume he got that from the sperm donor.

"Oh my, look what the cat dragged in, finally decided to please us with the presence of Van Gogh?" Ash snickers from behind his canvas.

"Keep it up, and I'll cut my ear off and staple it to your work."

"Do that, and I'll staple your balls to your forehead."

"You kiss your mother with that mouth?" I slump in my chair.

"Fuck no, that bitch probably has a disease. I'm sure she's cheating on Prescott, by the way."

I pick up a paintbrush, spinning it in between my fingers. "Yeah, I had that feeling too. Poor guy, I don't like him, don't get me wrong. But no one deserves to be cheated on."

I scan the room, my eyes landing on the bowl of fruit. I hate this class.

The nerd that Jinx is friends with sits directly across from me; I still want to beat the shit out of him. Now that

I'm moving into the same building as Jinx, I'll have unlim-
ited access to her. I almost lost my shit when Maddox told
me he spent the night with her. Damn, near put my fist
in his face. Of course, it would be him to spend the night
out of all of us.

I can't waste any more time. I need to make Jinx mine.

Okay, moving sucks. Even if it's only a duffle bag or
two, it still sucks. Room 418 is officially ours. It's almost
like Maddox's place, except the bedrooms are on either
side of the living space, and we have a shared bathroom.
It's way nicer than sharing with the swim team. Although
Nolan and Winston aren't bad, I can't stand the other
ones.

With nothing more to do, I might as well join the rest of
humanity in the food court, and it's still weird how things
are run here. It is very strict, almost like you're in prison.
Whoever owns this place has some control issues.

I take the path next to the trees; it's always been a
favorite of mine. The darkness calls to me more than
anything when I walk by. I notice a certain raven-haired
beauty staring into the tree line. When the wind picks
up, her body shivers. The rustling leaves tumble over my
boots as I walk closer.

"Scared?"

Jinx jumps, spinning around and meeting me with a small terror on her face.

"No." She side-eyes the trees.

I cock my head to the side. "You sure? Looks to me you are." I creep closer.

The closer I get, the more she steps backward. I love playing this game. It's a game I don't think she's ready for.

"What do you want, Atticus?"

A devilish smirk slips across my face. "I'm sure you can figure out what I want, Jinx. The question is, do you want it?"

The answer passes over her face. Oh, she wants it, but she's fighting it. She's looking for an out, a way to distract me. My little grim, that won't work. I'm on to you.

Her little huff seals her deal. "If you want me, you better come catch me." Her emerald eyes stare deep into my blue ones.

I chuckle. "Oh, Jinx. Those aren't smart words to say to me right now. But I'll give you to the count of five, and you better be gone. You better pray to God that I don't find you. Because when I do, I don't care what you say. I'm not stopping."

I back away. "One."

She doesn't move a muscle; her chest rises faster.

"Two, best start running."

She finally turns and takes off for the woods. It's a surprising place to run, but I'll take it. Why is chasing the woman that you want such a massive turn-on? My cock grows hard as I think of how I want her begging under me, all covered in dirt. I take off after her, and she won't get far. I have seven inches on her.

I hear her scream out in pain, turning left until I see her lying on the ground, clutching her head. I watch her freeze when I accidentally step on a stick, snapping it.

"Don't be fooled, little grim. I can smell you." I move into the clearing.

She shuffles back, hitting my legs.

"Five. Time to play," I snarl. Reaching down, I grab her hair, pulling her onto her knees. "I've waited a long time for this, and I'm surprised you did too."

"I didn't keep it for you, you asshole."

I tug harder, making Jinx whimper. "I love that sound from you. I wonder what other sounds I can get out of you?" Releasing her hair.

I don't know what it is about Jinx that brings out my dominant side, but fuck it makes me insane. I can't control myself around her. I want to ruin her but protect her altogether.

I brush the hair away from her face. "This can work two ways. You let me in, or I force my way in. Which way do you want it?"

She spits in his face. "Neither."

With one shove, she lands on her back. I truly admire the way Jinx dresses. Short skirts and her fishnets are my favorites. I glide my hands under her skirt, feeling the heat pour off her pussy. I press my finger over her clit before ripping her fishnets open. She screams.

"Yes, scream. No one can hear you." I rip her thong off before my fingers drive into her pussy. "Fuck, little grim, you're so wet for me."

Her face turns red—her needy moans fill the clearing. She's holding back; I can feel it. Her body is stiff, shoving another finger deep inside; she is so tight I can't wait to bury my cock in this hole. She tries to move away.

"You fucking take it. Get ready for my big cock. I'm gonna fuck you until you are bleeding all over this ground, I want to hear you scream, and those screams will turn into moans. You hear me?"

"Ah, I can't. It's too much already."

I wrap a hand around her throat, squeezing, making her submit, and tearing her shirt open, exposing her perfect breasts. I let out a groan as her nipples harden from the air.

"God, such a beautiful sight."

I forcefully grab one of her breasts, making her cry out. She bucks her hips, trying to escape. Little does she know, she can't escape. I can't let that happen; my world would be dark again. She continues to squirm, and I take a nipple into my mouth, biting it. Her body goes still under me.

I release her throat and watch her drag a deep breath in. When our eyes connect, she can finally tell the Atticus that she once knew is long gone. This one only cares about one thing. Jinx watches my hands move to my waistband as I flick open the buttons of my pants. This is one gift I've been waiting for her to see. I pull out a very hard and a very tattooed dick.

"Jesus Christ," she whispers.

I kneel between her legs, pushing them apart. Her pussy is waiting for me. I line my cock up and thrust in without any warning. Her body tenses, core tightening; she tries to push me away, but that only makes me drive all the way in, pushing past her hymen. She lets out a soundless scream, tears rolling into her hair. It only turns me on even more. I grab her hips and fuck her hard and fast.

"God, your pussy is tight. I knew the wait would be worth it. Aren't you glad you waited for me?" I groan. Thrusting deeper into her sore pussy.

She screams when I lift her hips, getting to the best spot. Her core clamps down on my cock, squeezing me so tight I swear she can break me. I spill a needy moan, filling my ball tighten into my body. I'm not ready to finish, but I can't help it.

"I'm coming, little grim." I flick her clit until she cries, gushing liquid everywhere. Well, shit, that's the hottest thing I've ever seen. My girl can squirt.

I pull out, look down, and grin. "Beautiful. You belong to me now. Don't get me wrong; I'll share you, but only with Ash and Mad. No one else, or I'll kill them." Standing, I tuck my bloody dick back into my pants.

That's my trophy for tonight.

She tries to cover up with what's left of her shirt. "If you're finished, you can leave now."

"Never. I would be a fool to leave now." I extend a hand. "Up. We should get going."

When she doesn't move, I release a harsh breath. I reach for her hand, pulling her up. I pull my hoodie off, tugging it over her head. Her body swims in it. When I let go of her, she wobbles. I quickly grab her waist.

"Guess I might have been a little rough."

"You can leave. You got what you wanted, didn't you?"

"Don't act like you didn't enjoy yourself back there."

She stumbles over a root, going down hard.

"Shit, Jinx. You gotta watch where you're going." I move next to her hands.

"Back off. I have other things on my mind, thanks," Jinx snaps, glaring up at him. "It's not always about you."

She starts to get up, but I'm an impatient man. I lift her over my shoulder.

"Atticus, put me down, you big oaf."

"No, if I do that, you'll fall again. Besides, my legs are longer than yours. So, will you tell me what's on your mind?"

She's silent, and I feel her fold her arms under her chest. But that's fine, and I have a nice view of this sweet ass. I smack it, getting her attention.

"The dorms are coming into view anytime you wanna talk. This would be it."

"Put me down. Everyone will see."

"Let them, at least they know you belong to me. What better way to show off my girl? Don't you think?"

This campus will know by morning who she belongs to. Her name will be all that's talked about.

Nineteen

Jinx

I can't sleep. My body is beyond sore, and I knew what I was getting myself into when I started running. Atticus warned me that if I did run, he would chase me. I never knew that I would be so into it. I wanted to fight him off; I wanted to scream no. But I was so far gone I enjoyed every single minute of it.

I craved it just as much as he did, if not more. What is wrong with me? It was downright dirty, don't get me started on his tattooed dick. Holy fuck, that was the hottest. I heard a lot about pierced dicks, but inked ones. Wow. It's phenomenal having a colored dick going inside of you.

See, without a doubt, there is something morally wrong with me.

I crawl out of bed, flinching with the first step. This week is going to be torture knowing that Atticus has gotten what he's wanted. I'll never get away from him. He's been waiting since he moved in, and I asked for help. I knew then that I should've saved myself.

My mind goes back to *Unknown. It's* been a week since I've heard anything from him, which makes me nervous. They could've seen Atticus and me in the woods yesterday. It also doesn't help that Atticus carried me back the entire way with me on his shoulder.

I might as well strap a neon sign to my ass and broadcast my every move.

Pulling Atticus' hoodie off the back of the couch, I inhale the scent of cigarette smoke and cinnamon. It's comforting knowing that he took care of me afterward. I thought for sure it would've been a fuck-n-dump. He insisted on drawing me a warm bath when he brought me back. A softer side of him I had never seen before, and I'll say I loved it.

Greywood Hall is going to be my undoing. Sign-up forms for the first concert were posted online, and I jumped at the opportunity to fill it out. I didn't pay much attention to who else was going. Perhaps that's my fault. I would've seen her name as the teacher's assistant.

Piper Day. That evil cocksucker herself. I'm sure she and Lula will battle out a schedule for Von's dick later.

How the hell did I not notice her name? If I had, I wouldn't have done this to myself. I grip the neck of my cello tight until the strings pinch my skin. Why can't my nightmares end already? These girls will never work hard for anything. All they gotta do is flash a little skin, and the men will bend over backward.

I need to escape; being in this room makes me feel ill. I suppose I could start working on my accounting work for business management. I'm over this, packing up my cello and getting a glare from Lula the whole time. She can shove it up her loose asshole. I don't need this; I have better shit to deal with. I trudge across the campus to the library. This place has always been my favorite spot. Walking up the steps, I'm greeted with the double wooden doors with carvings of ravens sitting in a giant oak tree.

Miss Phyllis barely acknowledges my presence—I'm used to it. I take the spiral staircase upstairs. The view overlooks the entire library, and hardly anyone comes up here. I take a table in the back, choosing the table with colorful patterns reflecting from the stained glass. I still remember when Dad took over the academy; this was my favorite hiding place. I would spend hours amongst the books, getting lost in the stories from the Grimm brothers.

I place my books down, determined to get my work done. For the life of me, I can't remember what possessed me to take this class. Accounting is hard.

"That vein in your forehead looks like it's about to burst."

My heart thumps wildly in my throat when I meet Ashton's eyes. The reflection from the window makes his eyes look like a kaleidoscope.

"God, your eyes are so beautiful."

"Thanks, sweet cheeks. I would love them if they didn't look like my mother's."

"At least they look like your brothers."

He shrugs, sitting in the chair next to me. "What are you working on." He grabs my books, groaning. "No, don't tell me."

"Yes, slacker. We have homework."

He blows out a long breath. "I'll make you a deal."

I groan, throwing my pen on the table. "Ashton, why don't I like the sound of this?"

"Oh, you will." He gives me that devilish grin.

He stands and disappears behind the bookcase. Whatever he's up to, I'm not going to like it. Ashton comes back, tossing up and down a chess piece. I side-eye him, waiting for him to tell me the plan. The bishop piece is placed on my paperwork.

"What am I supposed to do with this?" Raising my brow, I lift the piece.

"Oh, my little swan, it's not what you do with it. It's what I'm going to do with it."

Does he want to play chess?

"You do my work for me, and I'll make you come with this." The black bishop piece shines with so much mischief now.

He turns in his chair so his body presses against my arm. Wrapping his arm around my shoulder, he kisses my neck warmly.

"Spread your legs for me." Gliding his hand past my thigh-high socks and taps his fingers.

Waiting.

I need to start wearing pants again. I can't believe I'm doing this, but I swear these guys do things to me that I can't explain anymore. Thankfully, we're alone. Opening my legs, Ashton takes over from there.

"Homework, start it. Crunch those numbers, little swan." He takes the bishop, running it along my jaw. "Do you know what the rules of the bishop are?"

"Yes," I whisper.

"Good, at least you know there is no limit to where this bishop will go." Swiping it across my lips.

With a tap on the paper, I try to concentrate. It's even harder when his hand slides under my skirt and he rubs the bishop over my clit. I smack the desk, not expecting to feel such pleasure from a chess piece.

"Shh, don't make a sound. Good girls are rewarded. Are you going to be a good girl?"

A surge of electricity ran through my veins the more he moved the piece, opening my mouth to answer, only for a strangled moan to slip out.

He tsks. "I'm gonna have to punish you for that, little swan." He slips my thong to the side, slipping the bishop inside. "The torture is knowing that such a small item will have you on edge until you get the real thing again."

He pulls the bishop out, leaving it on the table, dripping in my wetness.

"You didn't make me come, so the deal is broken."

He stands. "You couldn't be quiet, so you need to be punished. I'll see you around, little swan." Then he casually strolls away. Leaving me feeling frustrated.

I swipe the bishop off the table, stuffing it inside my bag. I can't be here anymore. I pack all my books with no other place to go; I leave the library.

My phone dings with a text. Perfect timing, Spence. I dig it out, wondering what he's up to. He probably wants to grab something to eat.

Unknown: Amazing.

That's all it says—one word.

I stop dead, looking around the courtyard. So many students are on their phones. It could be any one of them. My heart races with the possibility of being watched. I try to swallow, but my throat has other ideas. I need to get back to my room before I have an attack.

Unknown: What's the matter, princess?

Tears impaired my vision immediately after reading that message. He's here. Drawing in a painful breath, I moved my untrustworthy legs. With each step, my chest tightened more and more. I'm only making it worse, re-thinking about everything.

I was stupid to think he would leave me alone—a week wasn't long enough. I checked. Ashton and I were alone. Where the hell was he hiding? Dear God, in behind the bookcases. That's the only spot he could've been.

My stomach churns like spoiled milk. I duck behind a tree and throw up my lunch. I stand, feeling sweat drip down my forehead, and my stomach threatens to heave again. I fumble with my fanny pack, and my fingers shake, trying to unzip this stupid piece of shit. My inhaler brushes my fingertips, and the sweet relief of breathing is near.

Unknown: You know, you should really check your sur-roundings better.

Why can't he leave me alone?

Me: Who are you?!

Unknown: Why would I tell you that? This is more enter-taining. The sight of you right now is such a turn-on.

I squeeze my inhaler tighter. No matter how much I want to look again, I don't. That'll give him so much satisfaction. Taking a puff, I keep hold of my inhaler.

I'm beginning not to trust this school. This was supposed to be my year. Why abruptly is it turning to shit? The back way to the dorm is less crowded but still busy. If anyone is on their phone, I should be able to remember them. Most of them are in my year. *Unknown* has got to be in my year. It would make the most sense.

I walk up the back steps, and my fingers brush against the handle when I'm grabbed from behind. I go to scream, but they're quicker, placing a hand over my mouth.

"Scream, and you'll regret it," there was an excited catch to his voice.

I try to fight, kicking at their legs, but nothing works. All he does is lift me and walk off to the woods. I scream into this hand, trying to grab anyone's attention.

My mind races. Did *Unknown* finally catch me? I'm not going to make it out of the woods in one piece. No matter how much I fight, his grip tightens around my stomach. I can't get my mind to think correctly.

It's the greedy moan that slips past his lips when my ass presses into his hard-on that I know his true intentions. I'm not letting this creep put his hands on my body. Throwing my head back, I smack him in the mouth. His hands slip, and I tumble to the ground.

When I look up, I can't believe it.

Twenty

Jinx

I can't believe I let myself think that this was happening. I need to get control of myself; I'm only freaking myself out. I stare up at him, only growing madder by the minute. When his lips turn up in a smirk, I lose it.

"Are you kidding me?" I push him back. "What the hell were you thinking?"

Atticus grabs my hand. "I was thinking of fucking my little grim again."

"Let go, Atticus," I say in a soft voice. "Please."

He stares into my eyes for a moment, looking for something. Instead of letting go, he pulls me into his chest.

"What's wrong? Something happened."

I try to turn away, but he tilts my chin up.

"Answer me, Jinx. What the fuck happened?"

I can't tell him about *Unknown*. I'm not sure what would happen if I did. Would he think it was my fault that another man was texting me? Atticus was adamant about me being his.

"I had a panic attack, that's all." He places the back of his hand on my forehead. I jerk away. "I'm fine, Atticus."

"You're not, Jinx. Come."

He practically drags me out of the woods. I watch as he digs into his pocket, pulling his phone out. I ignore him, going back to watching our surroundings. I don't trust *Unknown. He* could still be out here, watching, waiting. The sooner I'm back in my room, the better.

My skin crawls with the thought of him still being out here some place. I'll never find peace again if I don't find him. I'm hoping with Atticus showing up that, he scared *Unknown* away.

Atticus scoops up my bag, inhaler, and phone once we reach the door.

"I'm sorry about scaring you. Are you sure nothing else is bugging you? You're still a little pale." The worry on his face has turned up a notch.

When I meet his eyes, I give him a tired smile. "I'm fine, I swear."

"Not good enough. We're headed to my room."

He brushed his knuckles down the side of my face. The softer side of Atticus has my stomach in knots. He moves his hand to the middle of my back as we walk up the stairs.

I need to change the subject or do anything to keep him from asking questions.

"Are you enjoying living here instead of the house?"

"You wouldn't believe it, but I hated living with the team. Cameron thinks he's the fuckin' king, and I can't stand that shit. He needs to be knocked down a peg or two. Fuckin' douche."

"Ahh, yes, he does have that effect on people."

"What about the others? Know much about them?" he asks.

He enters the code to his room. "Emery is here on a scholarship. He wants to be just like Cam. Liam is a legacy student. I'm sure it was his great grandfather that was the first. And for Shane, I'm not entirely sure."

He whistles low. "Do I want to know how you know all this?"

I sit on the couch. "I've been here longer than you remember."

"Don't remind me, Jinx. Those were the worst two years that we had to go through."

"Yes, you keep reminding me. Can I go home?"

The sweet Atticus is gone, and I'm over it. It's like a light switch, and I can't keep up with the mood swings. I watch his eyes darken, leaning over me and pushing me further into the cushions.

"I'll keep reminding you until you never leave me again, Jinx." His face inches closer until his lips are next to mine. "I need you more than you know."

Our lips smash together, and the neediness never seems to end. He works his hand up my skirt, tugging my thong off.

"I'm getting a taste of this pussy. Spread your leg."

He moves fast; his head is between my legs before I can react. His hands gripping my thighs tight. I feel his hot breath on my clit before he licks a long stroke from my wet entrance to my clit.

"Atticus." I moan.

He moans, sending shockwaves up my body. My hand flies to his hair, pushing him deeper into me. He nips, sucks, and licks, sending me closer to the edge.

"Fuck, little grim. You're so beautiful when you're getting close. What about if I sent you closer."

He sticks a finger deep in, fucking me fast. My core tightens around his finger, my stomach clenching tight.

"I'm coming. Please don't stop." I'm almost there when he withdraws his finger. My body sagging on the couch in disappointment. "What the hell!" I pant.

"I don't want you to come yet." He stands and walks away without another word.

I can't believe he left me. What the hell was that all about? I knew he was an asshole, but to do that to me? That's a low blow. I grab my thong off the floor and get up to leave. Ashton appears out of nowhere.

"Where the hell were you?"

He points behind him. "My room, why?"

I can't exactly be mad at him for what happened. If he stayed or walked with me, would *Unknown* send all those text messages like he did? I can't handle this for much longer. I'm going to lose my mind. Is this what *Unknown* wants?

"Jinx? What's wrong? What happened?"

"She had a panic attack earlier. That's what happened." Atticus appears back in the living room.

Ashton moves quickly, grabbing my arm. "Why? Was it from me? I didn't mean to do anything to you without your say so. If I did this, please, Jinx, I need to know."

Tears sting my eyes. "It wasn't you, I swear."

"I have a bath ready for you. Go relax for a while."

Ashton kisses my forehead before letting go of me.

I'm not sure what to do, but maybe being alone isn't the right move. Or honestly, I don't know what is the right move. I'm so far over my head that I'm not going to survive much longer. I need to find the old Jinx, she didn't give a shit what happened, and she wasn't scared of anything. Why would I be scared now?

I need to talk to Dad. The thing with Von is bugging me, too. Why is Piper back being his assistant when she isn't a student anymore? There are so many things going on that I can't explain. Why does he need two assistants? It's a little concert, not a full-fledged symphony. Jesus, today is the worst day ever. The only good thing is being with the twins.

Getting undressed, I sink into the hot water. Atticus even added lavender bubble bath. Trying to turn my mind off is a whole other level. I should be upstairs practicing my cello or working on my accounting assignment. I have so much shit to get down, and I feel like I'm running out of time. This isn't how I should be prioritizing my time.

I still need to search Shane's room and get a better look into that box in Cam's room. I think they have a swim practice coming up, and I can always do it then. The house would be empty, and one would know it was me. I can get a key from Dad's office. Unfortunately, Spence can't come along with me this time. He'll ask too many questions, and I'm not ready to answer them.

I can't tell anyone.

With my plan set in stone, I only need everyone to leave me alone.

"Jinx, you doing okay in there?"

"I'm fine, Ashton."

The door opens enough for his head to poke through.

"I'm just checking. You were quiet, and after what Ace told me, I want to make sure."

I extend a hand to him. He crosses the small area, kneeling beside me and taking my hand.

"Honestly, Ashton. I'm fine. I think it was a cross of a panic and asthma attack, and I worked myself up. That's all."

"I don't believe you." His eyes search mine.

I lift a shoulder. "Well, I'm sure what you want me to say."

"The truth. That would be a good start. From one liar to another, you can't hide it forever. It'll eat you alive until, one day, you feel like dying. I'm here for you, Jinx. But until you're ready, I can't help you."

"How long did it take before you almost gave up?"

"When Atticus found me on the bathroom floor, Jinx. I'm not letting that happen to you. How bad is it?"

"I'm not sure yet."

He dips his hands into the bath water, getting close to my face. "You think Atticus can be very possessive. You have no idea. I'm about to be your worst nightmare, little swan. Get out. I'm coming back to your place tonight."

"Excuse me?"

"I didn't stutter."

He backs away, waiting for me to get out. "Privacy would be nice?"

"You have three minutes, and then I'm back." He taps his wrist and then leaves the bathroom.

How the hell am I supposed to work my plan if he's going to be glued to my ass now? It's going to be tougher dodging Ashton spying on Cameron and Liam, all while trying to figure out who *Unknown* is. Plus, practice my cello and keep my grades up.

"Times up, little swan."

That is going to be my real problem—bossy men.

Twenty-One

Ashton

There's something off with Jinx. She can lie all she wants, but I'll figure out what the hell happened yesterday. There is no way she got a panic attack out of nowhere. Something or someone had to have said something to her; my guess is Cameron. That dick isn't quiet about how he feels about her. I guess the beating he received from Ace didn't teach him anything.

Today is the last swim practice before our meet this weekend. I should be nervous, but it feels like second nature after doing this for almost four years. The only shitty thing is that coach wants our grades to be top-notch. That's the thing I'm struggling with the most. I understand that this school is for the most elite assholes, but come on. I'm not going to succeed in life, so why try?

I have no plans for a successful life, and I don't know what I want to do outside of school. I'm still young; I have time to figure it out. Why do I have to do it now? Can't I just live in the moment and get into trouble, break the law, and then, in my thirties, make up for it? Prescott has different options for me. He wants me to get into business and get established in a well-paying job.

That's not who I am. I'm not sure who I am.

I do know one thing: Jinx needs me, and I won't rest until I uncover her secret. She's trying hard to cover that secret.

———

This art teacher can seriously go to hell, and I can't complete this assignment, my accounting, and the Bio one. I won't be able to pass everything and keep up with my swimming. I splatter some paint bullshit on the canvas and call it good.

Art is nothing more than interpretation, anyway. She can't fail me because it's not what she wants. I wait until everyone leaves the class before I hand it in.

"Ashton, what is this?"

"That, my dear teach, is Art. It's what you asked for. It's what I see when I look at my most inner self."

My canvas is black with red splatters everywhere. It's what I see when I think back to my darkest time. I thought I wouldn't see the end of it.

"I see. How am I to grade you on this without knowing why or what I'm looking at? It's just black paint."

"Yeah, it's my soul. Nothing but blackness. You can't fail somebody for what they see."

I can't explain this to her. It is what it is. Why does everyone need to see what isn't there? Some people are more damaged than others. I have more pressing things to take care of.

"Sorry, but I gotta go. Is this going to fail or not?"

She takes a deep breath. "It'll pass for now, but I need more next time. I can't keep passing mediocre work."

Whatever keeps me on the swim team works for me. I head out of the art room in search of a nerd.

I can't keep doing my work and keep an eye on Jinx. I wish there were two of me at times, and it would make my life easier. Where would one find a nerd? The library or that stupid café? I'm not even sure. Fuck it, the café it is.

I've never stepped foot in the Raven Bean. To be honest, I'm not one to drink coffee. The atmosphere here is way out of my element. It's dark and gives me a weird vibe. The barista plasters a fake smile on and happily takes everyone's order. No offense, but no one is that happy. It's almost robotic. Shivers run down my back.

I move away from everyone. I scope out everyone on their laptops, needing that one good nerd that can pass my grades for me. That's when I see him, the one who could do it. I stroll over to his table. When I got close, I slammed his laptop closed, causing him to jump.

"Oh, hey, Ashton. What can I help you with?"

"Archie, I need you to do me a favor."

I watch his throat move up and down. "Um, y-yeah, okay. What is it?"

"Bio and Accounting. I need you to finish my assignments and make me pass without the coach finding out."

"It'll cost you."

"I'm aware of how this works, Archie. Not my first rodeo. The money will be in your account after I get the assignments, not before. Understand?"

He nods.

"Good, I'm sure you can figure out what needs to be done. Don't contact me until they are finished." I turn to leave and catch a glimpse of Jinx leaving.

I didn't think she drank coffee, either. I pick up the pace and rush out the door, only to lose her in the crowd. Where is she off to in such a rush? I don't have time to run after her now; I need to get my ass to the pool.

The walk to the pool is calming yet stressful. I'm calm because I'll be in the water, and I'm stressing because Jinx won't be in the stand watching me swim. I would be relaxed knowing she's nearby, not alone doing God knows what. I knew leaving her this morning was a mistake; she was sleeping when I snuck out, so peaceful I didn't have the heart to wake her. Maybe I should've told her to get her ass to the swim practice.

Atticus is in the locker room, changed and waiting for me when I enter—looking grumpy as ever.

"What's up with you? Someone pissed in your Cheerios?"

"Something like that. Coach still won't let me swim unless I apologize to Cam. I didn't do anything wrong, but he won't listen to me. Cameron needs to disappear."

I shove my bag in my locker. "Just apologize and drown the prick. We're doing the 400 meters. No one would know the difference, and they probably figure he's a shitty swimmer and can't handle eight laps."

He laughs, banging his head on the locker. "I thought of that, but the coach will be watching my every move now. I'm screwed. If I don't apologize, I'm finished, Ash."

"He's watching you," I say, "not me. I can do something to him."

I'll come up with a plan to remove Cam without getting kicked off the team. I need Ace, too.

"I'll meet you out there." He grabs his hoodie, leaving me alone.

Me: We need to remove Cam.

Mad: Got it. Leave it to me.

Always rely on the damaged friend to come through for you. Whatever Maddox is going to do will work in the end. I'm going to focus on getting in the water and swimming with my brother.

The coach glares at me when I walk out. He and I have a love-hate relationship; he hates me, and I love to get on his nerves. It's been working for us for the most part. If only he would, I don't know, try to love me more. I do like to be loved softly every so often.

"Getting your studies done, Ashton?" Coach asks as I near the bench.

"Yeah, I'm working on it."

"They better be done before the practice, or you're finished."

I roll my eyes. "Yeah, I got it I said."

Does he not know who my stepdaddy is? Does no one understand who he is? I knew we should've changed our last names when we started here.

"Is Atticus swimming?"

"For now, he is. One more screw-up, and he's gone too." He walks away and blows his whistle twice—a warning to get ready.

Once that whistle blows, I dive into the water. Slicing through the water, pushing my body to go faster. Stroke after stroke, I pass Cameron, laughing in my head, knowing that he'll never be better than me. Atticus deserves to be captain, not some shitty assaulter.

I'm three laps ahead of everyone, feeling my swimmers high; I'm untouchable. I'm so pumped for this practice. I'm kicking Grovedale's ass—they have it coming, especially after what they did to me. I'll never forget that night. It's one of the main reasons why I haven't made any more moves with Jinx, and I have a tough time getting past what happened to me.

When I near the ledge to turn around, I'm bumped from the side, smacking my head off the wall. Growing dizzy, my body can't fight to stay afloat, and I drop like a brick to the bottom of the pool. My world grows dark the more I struggle to breathe. All I want to know is what cunt I need to kill from doing this to me.

I have questions, like why does it feel like somebody is driving all over my chest? Don't they know that's highly fuckin' rude? My next question is, why it feels like an ocean is in my throat?

I roll onto my side, coughing up water, groaning, and swearing.

"Ash, you okay?"

I sputter more water up. "No," I rasp. "What the fuck happened?"

"You nearly drowned."

"Nearly, I'm sure I did. What asshat did it?"

Coach stands there with his arms crossed, a grim look to him. "That I'm not sure of. No one caught sight of you until you were down for a while. It was chaos afterward."

"I'm going out on a limb here, coach. It came from the side, so figure that out." I get up and march to the locker room; only two dicks were on my side, Cam and Liam.

I wonder which one did it. My bet is on Liam—he's Cam's dick sucker. Everyone knows Cam can't do shit by himself, but why come after me? Is he scared of Ace? He should be now because Ace is going to be raging once I tell him who I suspect. Hopefully, Maddox came through on his end.

"I'm going to kill 'em."

Atticus continues to bitch even in the showers. Nothing I've said has calmed him down; letting him get it out of his system is best.

"That prick could've killed you, and you haven't said two words about it, Ash. What the fuck?"

"I'm waiting."

He pulls my curtain back. "Waiting. What are you a kid at Christmas? Santa isn't coming this year, little Timmy. Grow up and deal with this." The anger pours off his body.

"Ace, Maddox was only supposed to deal with Cam for you, but it looks like I'll have to amp that up. Now." I pull the shower curtain closed. "If you don't mind, some fuckin' privacy."

Revenge shall be sweet.

Twenty-Two

Jinx

Ever have those moments in life where things are going great, and then a volcano goes off, and hot lava pours all over everything, melting it to nothing and burning your world to the ground? I'm at that point.

Professor Von has now decided that we should have a partner instead of solo concerts. No offense, but why should I help you get a head in this industry when I've been working my ass off since I was a little girl. He needs to be fired; what a complete nut job, and I know who is pulling the strings on this idea.

Stupid Lula Leboux.

There's another person I need to deal with. My hit list is getting out of hand. Something needs to give, and only one person can fix all this. I hate going to him for my mini meltdowns, but Von needs to go.

The office is empty when I step inside. I don't think I've ever seen Florence leave her chair. Where has that little hipster gone, too? When I round the corner to Dad's office, I see why. Ear pressed to the door, our nosy little secretary is spying.

I clear my throat, almost causing her a heart attack.

Florence places her hand on her chest, squeaking. "Odette."

"Yep, what's going on in there?"

She flashes me a nervous smile and glances back at the door. "Serena."

"Shit, what bullshit is she saying now?"

Thankfully, Florence despises that woman as I do. Florence shoos me back down the hall.

"She came storming in here, huffing and puffing like she always does. Demanding that, she talks to Prescott. She barreled me over just to get to his office. That poor man, I don't know how he always deals with her." She squeezes my hand. "Sorry."

"I'm not sure either. I've been here for most of the marriage."

"Count your blessings. From what I always hear, it's horrible. Sorry, sweetheart. It's not my place to judge. Want me to call your dad and rescue him?"

"No, that's okay. I have another way to get to him." Leaving Florence, I storm down the hallway.

If Serena thinks she can control my dad, she's mistaken. She's a nobody, just a horrible evil stepwitch. I don't even stop to think about it. I fling open those doors and glare at Serena. She hardly reacts to my entrance.

"Dad, I need to speak with you alone," I continue to stare at Serena, drilling it home that she's not wanted.

"Odette, I wasn't expecting you."

"Yeah, sorry, it was a last-minute decision and, by the looks of it, a smart one. Leave Serena."

"Why, you little—"

"I dare you to finish that sentence, but we wouldn't want Dad to see what a bad person you are now, would we."

"Prescott, are you going to let her talk to me like this?" Her nasally voice makes my teeth clench.

Dad sighs. I can't help it. The witch gets on my nerves, but he has to come to terms with the fact that she's only with him for the money.

"Serena, I'll see you at home."

She huffs, getting up. "Unbelievable." Brushing my shoulder on her way out.

"Cunt," I mumble.

"Enough, Odette. Now, what is it that you need?"

I slump into the chair, taking in his odd décor. People think I'm the weird one in the family. Unfortunately, I got that from my father. Embrace the weirdness. If you don't, then who will?

"It's about Von."

"Odette, I can't, and you know it. I've tried searching for a replacement. I can't find one."

"He hired outside help, his student from last year, that can't be legal."

He leans back in his chair, rubbing his chin. "It's not. He knows better. What is he up to?" The phone rings, interrupting his thoughts.

"Dean Hawthorne."

I watch as Dad's face falls, and he continues to listen. Now, my radar is on high alert, leaning forward, trying to listen to whoever is speaking. Whatever happened, Dad looks pissed. That means it occurred on campus.

"Sweetheart," his voice softened as he hung up. "Ashton had an accident during his swim practice."

My hands tremble, and I tuck them under my legs before Dad can see them. "How? What happened?" I force my voice not to break.

"The coach wasn't sure, exactly. All he told me was he hit his head and went under. The lifeguard was the one that pulled him out." He straightened to his full height. "I'm going to go check on him. Did you want to join me?"

"Yeah, I need to head back and practice." I pick my bag up as he guides me out of the office.

"I'm proud of you, kid. Can you imagine if you still wanted to play the bass?" He chuckles.

I groan. "That was a painful day, and I'm not sure my shins ever recovered from getting the crap banged out of them. I don't know what I was thinking."

"You've always been ambitious, Odette. That's what I love about you. Let's see what your brother has to say about what happened today. I'm serious about this school going to shit. It's like someone is out to get me, I swear."

"Don't say that."

It's already getting dark, and to be frank, I'm glad Dad is walking me back to the dorms. I sound like a giant scaredy cat when I should start trying to figure out which asshole tried to kill Ashton. It had to be someone on his team. If it weren't for the lifeguard, he would be—nope. Not thinking about that.

"What will you do once you discover who did this to Ashton?" I open the door to Darrow Hall.

Dad stares into my eyes. "I would love to murder that son-of-a-bitch, but that's frowned upon. It'll land in law enforcement's hands. We should hurry. I have to let Serena know soon."

Ugh. She'll make a big stink about it and then insist on returning to the campus. I can't see her again. Oh, wait. I don't have to. Not my mother.

———

Ashton is resting on the couch when we enter, pale as a ghost. I watch as Dad checks him over. The lump on the side of his head doesn't look so hot, and I can't imagine the headache that comes along with it.

"Are you sure you don't want the doctor?" Dad asks again.

"Yeah, I'm good. I took some pain meds. I want whoever did it found so I can beat the shit out of them."

"We'll find them, Ash." Atticus paces around the small kitchen. "Like you said earlier, it could only be two people, Cameron or Liam."

Dad moves to the door. "I'll deal with those two in the morning. Get some rest, and I'll make sure your professors know you'll be out of class tomorrow." With a final wave, he walks out, leaving me alone with the twins.

I turn back to Ashton, crossing my arms. "Tell me, what the hell went down for this to happen?"

"Atticus happened. They wanted an apology, and we all know how that went down."

"Fuck them, I'm not apologizing, and they can forget about it now. I should go over there and kill them."

"No need. Maddox has already taken care of Cam, but Liam, we need a plan to take care of him."

I sit on the couch, trying to process everything. "Hold on, what did Maddox do to Cam?"

Ashton laughs, then winces. "Fuck." Placing a hand on his head. "Maddox is the firebug, little swan. What does Cam love more than anything in this world?"

"His car."

"Ah-uh. That poor car is currently on fire in the parking lot. Expect step-daddy to call us any minute when the fire trucks show up."

Jesus Christ, these guys have barely been here for a month and are already causing havoc on the place. Is it their mission to destroy relationships every place they go? If they keep this up, no one will want anything to do with them.

"What happens when this blows back on you?"

"It won't," Atticus tells me.

"If you say so, but I should be going."

Ashton sits up, grabbing my hand. "Not so fast, little swan. I'm in need of a nurse."

"I'm not going to be your nurse. Get your brother to do that."

He runs his hand up my thigh. The closer he gets to my pussy, the wetter I become.

"I love how you look at me when you're turned on."

I shouldn't want this—them. My brain says one thing, and my body tells me something different. Which is a little late, considering what Atticus and I did in the woods earlier.

"Ashton, we can't."

"Oh, we can't, but my brother can."
He pulls me onto his chest with a grin.

Twenty-Three

Jinx

My mind is blank. Ashton wants me to do what in front of him? I'm sorry, but I'm not sure what to do anymore. I think Ashton was hit harder than expected if he thinks I'm fucking his brother in front of him.

Atticus moves behind me, his hand working under my shirt. "Arms up, little grim."

His breath blows across my neck, sending chills throughout my body. My arms lift with no hesitation, and he hums as his hands slowly lift my shirt higher. Ashton brings his hands to my breasts once they are free.

"I love that you never have to wear a bra. Your breasts are perfect." Ashton tugs at my nipples, arching my back and pressing my breasts more into his hands.

"I think my brother needs some medical attention. Do you know how to heal him, Jinx?" Atticus asks.

"No."

"Sit on his face and let him eat that magical pussy of yours."

With shaky legs, I stand, pushing my pants down. I stand in only my black underwear. Both guys let out a needy groan when they see the tattoo on my hip. Atticus traces it with his finger.

"When did you get this?"

The treble clef stands proud for only those who are allowed to see it. Those who know me know the reason behind it. "I was in high school still. Shortly after you two recovered my cello from those bitches, I went out later that week and got this."

Atticus stares hard at it before he tugs my underwear down.

"Fuck, I missed this pussy." He runs his finger along my lower lips. "Ash, get her nice and wet for me."

Ashton holds his hand out for me, and without thinking, I take it. Sealing in my fate.

My thighs rest on either side of his head, and I stare down at him. His blue eyes are blown out in ecstasy. "Tell me if I hurt your head, and I'll get off."

"The only getting off you do is with my tongue." His fingers dig into my skin. "Now sit." He growls.

I barely sit, and he attacks my clit with his tongue, licking, sucking, and biting. My hips rock the more he flicks at my clit. Atticus reached around, cupping my breasts, pressing me close to his chest.

"It makes me so horny watching my brother eat you out, little grim. Does it feel good?" he asked, a note of firmness to his voice.

I opened my mouth to answer, but all that came out was a small cry when Ashton picked up the pace with his assault on my clit. My legs shake, and I lay my head on Atticus' shoulder; my breathing picks up.

"Ashton, please. I need to come," I demand greedily.

I'm lifted in the air, the rush of pleasure hanging in the air, my pussy throbbing with need.

"I could spend all day between your legs, but Ace needs you now. Come for him, little swan, come nice and hard."

Atticus places me on the cushion facing the kitchen. Spreading my legs wide, he smacks my pussy.

"I can't wait to fuck you again. Although it's exciting when you're running, this will have to do."

I glance over my shoulder, watching him pull his shirt off over his head. I'll never get tired of seeing all of his tattoos. It's when his pants drop that I go breathless again. That tattooed dick of his will be the death of me. He runs his fingers along my clit before smacking it.

"Oh, fuck." I grip the edge of the couch. I side-eye Ashton, watching his hand disappear under his sweatpants.

Atticus' warm body embraces mine, causing my back to arch, driving my ass into his dick.

"Yes, little grim. Get ready to be fucked fast and hard. You made me wait longer than I wanted to. Let's make Ash jealous."

With a rough thrust, he drives deep inside of me. I bite the couch, screaming. Atticus pulls my hips into him, ramming his hips into my ass. I'll admit this is better than the first time, but he's still so intense.

"Yes, squeeze my cock. Who owns this pussy?" He fucks faster.

"Y-you do."

Heat spread through me, and his breath came harder and faster.

"Who will I share you with?" Pounds with no remorse.

Ashton groans next to me, making my toes curl. "Ashton and Maddox," I finally say.

"Good girl, no one else touches you."

My body shakes, and a knot of emotion burns in my center as I come hard. Atticus groans, coming deep inside of me. Sweat trickles down my spine, I try to control my breathing, but nothing seems to work. I bend over, coughing hard.

"Jinx, are you okay?" Ashton rests his hand on my back.

I try to talk, but only wheezes come out.

"Shit, her inhaler, grab it."

I wonder who I pissed off in the past life to be blessed with asthma, especially to get an attack after sex. How sexy is this that I can't even get my brains fucked out of me? I need to talk to the doc again. This is bullshit.

"Here, Jinx. No dying on me today." Atticus pops my inhaler in my mouth.

After a few puffs, my chest already begins to loosen up. Ashton pulls me into his chest while Atticus covers me up.

"Shh, get some rest. We'll be here when you wake up. Nothing will happen while you're in my arms, little swan."

"This wasn't how I wanted it to go, and I'm supposed to be nursing you, Ash."

His chest rocks me with his silent laugh. "You've never called me Ash before. I like it."

"It's better than what I call you both behind your back."

"Do I want to know?" Atticus asks.

"The Shining Twins." I laugh.

Atticus sighs. "Lovely."

"To be fair, you did play with us," Ashton mutters in my ear.

I bury my nose into his neck, breathing in his fresh scent. It's one thing that I'll never get tired of.

Waking up warm and with a body pressed against me on either side isn't what I want. Okay, I don't know what I want. But this could be it. I'm not good with this. I had a goal, and these two are ruining everything. At least with Maddox, he sticks to himself unless I need him. My heart aches for him. I want my strong Maddox back.

"What's got you thinkin' so hard this early?" Atticus breathes into my neck.

"I was thinking about Maddox."

Ashton rubs my hip, his lips gently kissing my neck. "Maddox is complicated. I'm sure you know this, it's hard for him to trust others."

"I want him to open up more, and I'm trying everything to be there for him."

"Give him time, little grim."

"He'll open up when he's ready, little swan."

I don't want to rush him, and giving him his own space is what I should be doing, but I feel like I need to be doing more. He doesn't have anyone in his life looking out for him except the twins. At least I had Dad growing up; the twins had their evil mother. From what I gathered, Maddox's parents were never there. He would never tell me, but I'm not stupid—I figured it out. He never talked about them. He was always at our house, and his mood shifted tremendously by the time graduation came.

"I think I'm going to go see him. Something has been bugging me for a while now."

Ashton rolls me onto his chest, wrapping his arms around my back and holding me tight.

"Why all of a sudden are you interested in us? I thought you wanted to stay far away from us."

I'm not sure what changed. I still want some distance from them all, maybe not all the time now. The more I spend time with them, the more I begin to fall for them. Can I be falling for three guys? Oh my God, I am.

"Jinx, what's wrong?"

I roll off him, getting out of bed. "Nothing. I have to go."

Atticus sits up with a scowl on his face. "No."

I freeze. "Excuse me? You can't tell me what to do."

"I'm sure I can. I said no. We'll go with you to see Maddox. You want answers. He'll give them more if we are with you. I know exactly the answer you want the most." He touches his jaw.

I'm curious who wouldn't be. I don't want to put Maddox in a position where he has to be forced to tell me about what happened. It has to be on his terms; maybe having the twins there will be a good thing.

One thing I know about Maddox is that he won't come to us for help.

The next best thing is for us to go to him.

Twenty-Four

Maddox

I'm glad I don't have morning classes; my body can't function, and the twins have their meet on Saturday. After what I did to Cameron's car, shit is about to hit the fan. Prescott is going to know it's me; it's only a matter of minutes until my phone goes off. That's why I'm spiraling, and I'm not sure how to get back. The darkness is slowly creeping in, and I can't find the will to fight anymore. Every day is a battle that I'm afraid I'm going to lose. What's the point of going on if I can't? I thought coming here would be better and that I would magically be better.

That was a bunch of bullshit.

Insomnia has hit me hard for the last couple of days, and I'm patiently waiting for my brain to cave and shut the hell up and finally crash. Apparently, drinking and smoking aren't doing the trick anymore. I have officially grown accustomed to the ways of the liquor—I need something harsher.

I think there might be something in the bathroom. I packed emergency pills for situations like this. Standing up from the couch, the room spins—I hate the spins. If there were a way to drink and not feel this, that would be the way to do it. I slowly stagger to the bathroom, gripping the doorframe, when my body betrays me and begins to fall.

The wall, however, does feel nice and cold, closing my eyes, I enjoy it momentarily.

"Mad, where you at?"

Perfect, just what I needed. A witness to my downfall.

Gentle hands cup my cheek, and I open my eyes, not an ounce of pity in her green eyes, and that breaks me. My knees gave out, taking us to the ground, burying my head into Jinx's neck.

"I'm here for you. Nothing will touch you," Jinx said in what was almost a whisper, nearly breaking me more.

Two more bodies press against me, spreading strength into me. I will myself not to cry, and it's hard not to.

"Talk to us. What do you need?" Ash talks first.

I breathe deeply, trying to find the words, but nothing comes out.

"Start from the beginning."

Jinx wraps her arms around me, holding me tighter. She smells like coconut—it's soothing. I've never felt like this before. The thought that somebody actually cares about me sends my heart in an outrage.

"I'm not sure. I was fine all night. I did what Ash wanted me to, and then I just." I move away from Jinx, looking at Ace and Ash, shaking my head.

"It's all right." Ace pulls me into his arms. "I've got you, brother. Always."

"It's getting harder every day, Ace. I can't do it." It's getting harder to speak with the lump forming in my throat.

"That's why you have us. Don't ever be afraid to call. Yeah?" He pushes me back, his eyes raking mine.

I nod in agreement. "Yeah, I'll try."

Jinx stands, extending her hand out. Her lips smiled slowly, and my heart skipped a beat. She's my missing puzzle piece. I still can't be hers. Who wants this mess of a person to always be in their life?

"Take my hand, Maddox. I'm not leaving."

I finally take her small hand, hauling myself off the floor. "You are hard to say no to, baby." I fist her hair, pulling her closer to me. "You drive me crazy."

"Good." She lifts up on her toes, pressing her lips to mine. "I did want to talk to you, but perhaps another day. Want some breakfast? Sure you do. Atticus, go grab some food."

Ashton laughs from behind me. "You heard the lady. Chop, chop."

"I hate all of you," Ace grumbles, leaving us.

"I'm surprised he listened to you, little swan."

Atticus will do anything for Jinx, fuck, we all will.

———

Sitting around my small ass table, eating whatever Ace could find in the food court, is interesting. I sometimes forget what it's like to sit around with a family. For the longest time, it was always just me. Even spending time at the Banks residents, it wasn't like this. Serena was always gone looking for the next husband. When she found Prescott, we all won the jackpot. Atticus hated Prescott, I'm not sure if he still does now, but I will forever be grateful to that man.

He took me aside after the first week of me showing up every single day and told me that I could take the spare bedroom whenever I needed it, no questions asked. I knew it killed him that I wouldn't tell him what was going on, and I regret that I never did. The second I turned eighteen, I moved out of my shithole of a house and never looked back.

"Maddox, walk me back to my place, please." Jinx places her hand on my shoulder, dragging me out of my thoughts.

"Uh, yeah. You two assholes, don't make a mess." I point at the twins.

Ash laughs. "The place is already a mess."

"Then clean it," I mumble on the way out.

Jinx is waiting for me in the hall, smiling like she always does when she sees me. Even after our reunion, when I wasn't nice, she still never gave up on me.

"How are you feeling?" Her hand slips into mine as we reach the stairs. "And don't say *I'm fine.*"

"Overwhelmed."

"I figured that's why I pulled you away. Besides, you haven't seen Edgar in a while. He's getting better much faster than the vet said he would."

I wait for her to enter her door code. "Well, he does have you nursing him back to health."

"I only feed him treats." She answered with a laugh.

Edgar sings out when we step inside her dorm, hoping around the floor.

"He sorta flew the coop, so I gave up on the box. Edgar is a free spirit."

I kneel in front of him. "Come here, buddy." Scooping him up, I walk him to the counter. "Are you giving Jinx a hard time?"

Gwah, Gwah

"I see. It's easy to do. It's my favorite thing, too." Finding his treats, he quickly chows down. Turning to Jinx, she's grinning. "What was the question you wanted to ask earlier?" I watch as her grin disappears. Ah, shit.

"I'm only asking if you are comfortable answering. There is no pressure." She bites her lip. "It's a personal question, Maddox."

I have a feeling I know where this is going. Not only do I have scars on the inside, but the one on my face is like a beacon in the dark. Always shining light and casting people's stares. I understand why she wants to know, and it's not to make me feel like a piece of shit. I nod in the direction of the couch. This is a sit-down conversation.

My eyes fixate on the faded spot on the floor. Slowly releasing a breath, I speak, "After you left, I didn't know what to do with myself. I found myself in some trouble, and I thought going to college would straighten me up—sadly, I was wrong." My hands tremble when I remember that night.

College wasn't something I was looking forward to. But Prescott somehow found a scholarship for me, or so he says. Who in their right mind would give me anything? I enrolled in what I thought was the greatest music program; it turns out it was garbage. The teacher, or whatever she thought she was, lacked talent. Half the kids in there didn't give a shit and goofed off half the time.

Halfway through the semester, I was given a chance to play at a concert of a lifetime. I was over the moon excited. Finally, somebody was giving me a chance at something. The night before, I stayed behind late to practice, wanting to make sure I was perfect.

Little did I know I was followed by the two biggest cunts in the program. They were jealous that I won the spot; they had a massive hard-on for the teacher. Evidently, sticking your dick inside of her didn't pay off.

"Well, if it isn't the golden student." Trent snickers when I step outside.

"Fuck off, asshole. I'm not in the mood." I watch Bradley move behind me.

"You think you are better than us, is that it? Bradley scoffed. His hands land on my back before pushing me forward.

Trent and Bradley both laugh low with malice. Turning fast, I swing at Bradley, nailing him in the mouth.

"You fuckin prick." He spits blood out, shaking his head. "You'll regret that."

Trent moves faster than I expected, grabbing my arms and pinning them behind my back. Two against one, not looking great. A slight clicking sound brings my eyes to Bradley's hand.

A switchblade.

I struggle to get out of Trent's hold. The closer Bradley gets, the more my heart tries to beat out of my chest.

"Every time you look in the mirror, you'll remember us. You'll remember how you stole this from us. I hope it was worth it."

"No, stop." My voice came out uneasy, and they caught onto that.

Trent's hold tightens as Bradley runs his knife along my jaw. A sharp, piercing pain shoots through my body.

"Hey, assholes. Get away from him!" Ash yells.

I watch Ace and Ash storm across the grass, picking up speed when they see me bleeding.

"Motherfucker," Ace growls. Driving his fist in Bradley's face, sending him to the ground.

I'm not sure where I would be if they didn't show up. Chances are I would've ended up with more scars. I ended up getting thirty stitches and a reminder that I'll never be good enough.

I stare at Jinx, tears rolling down her cheek.

"Those assholes ruined your chance because they were jealous. I'm so sorry, Maddox." She pulls herself closer, brushing kisses along my scar. "I'll never allow that to happen again."

"I can't let you promise anything, baby. There are some battles that I need to fight on my own."

Her eyebrow raises, and I know I'm never going to win them alone again.

Twenty-Five

Jinx

Saturday had finally arrived, and the twins begged me to attend their swim meet. I'm glad that Ashton is feeling better, but I'm still nervous that he'll have another accident today. The worst part is the meet is taking place in Grovedale.

That means dinner at the wolf's den after.

I wanted to bring Spence along, but I didn't want to torment him with all that. No one deserves that. Serena is unpredictable, and I adore Spence too much. And let's be honest, Spence will fly off the handle and say something he shouldn't.

Instead, Maddox is coming. I'm not sure how he feels about it because he hasn't said a word the entire drive.

His death grip on the steering wheel tells me everything I need to know; we share the same feelings.

"Do you think Ashton will be okay?" I finally broke the silence.

He exhales, squeezing the steering wheel until it squeaks. "God, I hope so. He seemed fine yesterday, with no concussion. I'm sure the coach will let him swim today."

That's not what I mean. Of course, the coach is going to let him swim today. He can't afford not to. Ashton is a strong swimmer, stronger than Cam. I have a feeling Cam caused Ashton's accident. I'll be keeping my eye out for him today.

"What about Cam's car? What happened there?"

He chuckles. "Your dad paid me a visit. Go figure that I would be the first on the list. I acted all innocent. I told him I had no clue what went on and said I was in my room the entire time practicing for music."

"And what about Cam? He's gotta be pissed."

"I'm not sure. Your brothers haven't mentioned it."

That's a little suspicious if you ask me. Cam loves that car, and not a single thing was mentioned anywhere around campus. It's like nothing has happened. Dad never even mentioned it to me.

Pulling into the Grovedale Community College parking lot seems weird, and I'm so used to staying at RWA that being anywhere else seems foreign.

"Did you like going here?"

"For the most part, it wasn't terrible. RWA is a lot better, that's for sure."

I jerk my head toward the campus. "I wouldn't know. I'm sure you know why I never wanted to come back. I don't regret my choices."

He threads a hand through his hair, slowly turning to meet my eyes. "I know the factors. Yes. I'm just glad to have you back."

As much as I fought having them back, I'm glad, too. They have a way of crawling deep under my skin, and getting rid of them is hard. I'll be the first to admit I caved quickly. Atticus should've worked so much more, but if we're telling the truth, I wanted him so bad, and I couldn't lie to myself anymore.

"Don't go far. I don't trust these people," he tells me before exiting the car.

"Wasn't planning on it." This college gives off bad mojo.

I thought RWA was dark and gloomy, but Grovedale is a different kind of gloom. This school looks like a kindergartner with some building blocks built it. Random heights, curves, and slanting roofs. They missed the mark if they wanted to go for a modern look.

The aquatic center is swarming with people by the time we reach it. Maddox hooks his finger around my pinkie, tugging me along with him.

"Did you want to sit with your dad?"

"To be honest, Serena is probably sitting with him. We can sit somewhere else. I'll tell Dad the plan."

I didn't think swim meets were so popular. Swim practices weren't this busy, so I assumed the meets wouldn't be. Man, was I mistaken. The bleachers are already packed full; you can tell which crowds are from where with the different colors they are wearing. I am not sporting our school colors, never have, and never will. The blue and gold are not for me.

"Have you been to one of the twins' meets before?"

"I've been to everyone, and it'll be crazy busy once they come out. Their fans will scream the roof down."

Lovely.

Maddox wasn't kidding. The entire place went up in roars when all the guys came out of the locker rooms. I've never seen so many speedos in my life. There was only one person that stood out the most.

Atticus Banks. His decorated skin is hard to miss. It also doesn't help when his piercing blue eyes devour me with one look. When Ashton steps next to him, meeting my eyes, I'm so screwed.

"Feeling okay, baby?"

"Uh-huh."

Maddox's fingers closed around my chin, angling my face to his. "Let them watch." He moved slowly, pressing his lips to mine.

Our lips moved as if we were hungry, and we would never have a moment like this again. His hand slides into my hair, pulling me closer and making him groan into my mouth, and I savor it. I finally release the kiss, breathless.

"Kissing you is my favorite thing to do, baby." Interlacing our fingers together, he brings my knuckles to his lips.

When I look back at the twins, I see that they each smile with satisfaction. I blow them each a kiss; Ashton reaches out and catches it, only for Atticus to smack the back of his head. I cringe, praying it doesn't affect the injury he already has.

The ref blows his whistle, and the first competition starts. I can't remember which one the guys are in. All I know is it's not diving. They both made a huge stink about that when they first started swimming and said it was for the brainless idiots. My gaze drifts to Cam and his loser friends as Liam climbs the ladder for the diving boards. I guess they were right.

"Can I ask you a question?" Maddox's voice pulls me away from Clam Jam.

"Of course. What is it?"

He rolls his shoulders. "It's about the upcoming concert. I signed up, and I'm not sure what to expect. Did I do the right thing?"

I practically bounce out of my seat. "Oh my God, yes! Maddox, this is the best thing for you. You finally get your chance to show everyone your exceptional talent. What's got you so nervous?"

I watch as he runs his finger along his jaw. Ah, fuck. I have no doubt he's scared because of what happened last time he wanted to try his hand at a concert. RWA is different. The only thing he has to worry about is the dicksuckers.

Maybe I have something to worry about.

"It's great that you believe in me, but would you be my partner?"

My heart sang. I've been waiting for this moment again. "Yes, Maddox. I would love to. You know it's my favorite thing. I love hearing you play."

He rests his hand on my thigh, content with my answer. We watch the swimmers, waiting patiently for the twins. When the ref announces the 800-meter relay swim, I watch the twins take their place. Who knew swimming could be so sexy?

Ashton dives into the water without missing a beat, and he's so fast that I can't keep track of him. Maddox is out of his seat, cheering him on. It's neck and neck with the other team from Grovedale. As he finishes his seventh round, Atticus dives in. Still in the lead, they make the perfect team.

I'm on the edge of my seat, watching as the other team gains on them.

Everyone from our school begins to chant louder; the more the clock grows, the more my anxiety increases. I have all the faith in the world that the guys will win, but it sure is gonna be a tight race.

"Don't worry, baby. They never lose." Maddox winks at me.

"Oh, I know. Trust me."

If it's one thing about the twins, losing isn't a word they believe in. They only ever see the finish line and coming in first. It's one reason why I didn't stand a chance.

I scream for Ashton to swim faster, and the hairs on my neck stand up—somebody is watching me. My eyes drift to where Cam is; surprisingly, it isn't him. I edge my hand into Maddox's, squeezing tight. I continue to scan the bleacher, but it's complicated with all these people. *Unknown* is here somewhere, and he's watching me.

"Hey, it's going to be fine. Ashton will win. Don't worry." Maddox squeezes my hand in return, not knowing the true meaning.

I try to smile in return, but I can't. I can't move at all, not even when Ashton wins. How did he know that I would come here? I wasn't even sure until the last minute.

"Jinx? What's wrong?" Panic settles in Maddox's eyes. Grabbing my hand, he hauls me through the crowd. We are barely outside when he cups my cheeks. "Tell me. I'm not letting you go until you tell me. This is the second time I have watched you go into a panic. What the fuck is happening?"

I place my shaky hands over his. "I'm scared."

"Scared of what?"

My phone dings in my fanny pack. I nervously take it out, not knowing who is texting me. Relief flows through me.

Ashton: Where are you?!

Me: Outside with Maddox. Why?

Ashton: I'll be out shortly for my winning kiss.

"Jinx, answer me."

"I can't say—"

"Fuckin lie to me again, and I'll smack that ass until it's blistering."

My eyes damn near bug out. Maddox has never talked like this before. I slowly start backing away.

"No way, baby. Get that ass back here. I'm not into fast food."

I keep backing up until I bump into a hard body.

"Where ya going, little swan?"

Maddox raises a challenging brow. "She was about to tell me something serious, but I think we'll wait for Ace to arrive."

Ah, shit. Now, there is no getting out of it. Atticus will do anything to get the information out of me, including letting Maddox smack my ass.

Twenty-Six

Jinx

I can't say I'm pouting, but I'm one hundred percent am—it's unfair.

Maddox placed me on the hood of his car and stood between my legs until Atticus arrived. No words have been exchanged except for my phone call to Dad, telling him we'll be late getting to the house.

Atticus takes a long drag of his smoke before flicking the butt to the ground. His dirty look doesn't help with wanting to spill my guts to them.

Atticus grips my chin tight. "I'm counting, Jinx, then you talk. I'm getting tired of waiting."

I draw in a long breath. "What does it matter to you?"

Ashton turns his back on me, Maddox squeezes my thighs, and Atticus could kill me alone with his look.

"Little swan," Ashton says, looking at me again. "If it wasn't clear how we felt about you, let me spell it out. Us three." He points to all three of them. "Will follow you to the end of the world."

"He's right. Whoever comes between us will not survive," Maddox adds.

Atticus still has my chin in a vice lock. "You will tell us." My phone dings, and I freeze. Atticus grins. "Retrieve the phone."

Maddox slips his hand into my pack, pulling my phone out, and his face turns red. "Who the fuck is this?"

He turns the phone to me, revealing a text message from *Unknown.*

My nightmare has been set free, and sweat slowly drips down my spine when I read my phone.

"No, little grim. Read it out loud."

My heart stumbled out of sync, and my words stuck in my chest. Bursts of air spew from my mouth rapidly, drying out my tongue like the dessert. Atticus shakes my phone impatiently, waiting. I cautiously take my phone, swiping it open. The text message comes to life, and I almost drop it. I bite back the cry when I reveal the picture of all of us.

I'm on the hood of Maddox's car with him between my legs, Atticus holding my chin, and Ashton with his back to me. *Unknown* is here right now.

I jump off the car, pushing Maddox and Atticus out of the way. I stumble over my feet, falling to the pavement, wincing in pain when the loose gravel scraps open my palms. I frantically scan every person, watching them get into their cars without paying attention to our group. There's no way that *Unknown* is watching us—it can't be true. Who would want to? I jump when a hand lands on my shoulder.

"It's only me, little grim." Atticus kneels next to me.

"We can't be here. We need to leave. Now," I tell him, looking around alarmed.

"Hey, look at me."

A car revs in the distance and my body becomes rigid—it's him, I know it. Atticus lifts me, carrying me to the car.

"We need to leave. She can't be here anymore. To the house, dinner can wait until we clear this up."

I tune out the rest of the conversation. My brain has officially gone on holiday. If *Unknown* wanted me to check out officially, he's getting his wish. I knew the guys should've stayed away. They just don't get the point.

"Don't worry, little swan. I won't let anyone hurt you." Ashton says, pressing me into his body.

"Ashton. I'm sorry I wasn't there when you came out of the locker room."

"Sweetheart, there is nothing to be sorry about," He spoke faintly, kissing my forehead. "I'll take a rain check, though."

"Only you would try to get laid right now."

"Oh, I don't want to get laid. I'll let you know when I do."

Ashton is layered thickly, even sitting in the back of the car; he only cares about me. Not once has he stopped caressing my inner thigh. The worst part is he's turning me on, and I need to keep my head straight. Not worrying about my throbbing pussy.

"Don't worry, little swan. I'll take care of you after you tell us what's been happening."

"Giving her a little incentive to spill the beans?" Maddox asks with a laugh.

"Whatever works to get that mouth to work," Atticus adds, his tone deathly serious.

Fuck, fuck, fuck.

Dad's house hasn't changed one bit since the last time I've been here. I still can't believe Serena hadn't made him renovate, considering she made him repaint every room when she moved in. She took over the entire house; it made me feel so unwanted.

I climb the stairs with the guys following close. Memories of me running up and down these stairs as a child flash in my mind; things seemed simpler when you were small and naïve. Maddox places his arm around my waist, guiding me to my old room.

Atticus opens the door, waiting for me to step foot in first.

"Sorry about your room when you didn't come home after the first year. Mom came in here," Ashton apologizes.

My room isn't my room anymore; it's set up as a guest room. "Wow, there was no question she wanted me gone. I'm surprised she waited a year." What a complete bitch. I should've known this would happen.

"Ah, we can go to my room if you want?" Ashton says, massaging the back of his neck, looking nervous.

It's cute how he gets nervous, but it's only a bedroom. "When did Atticus move out?"

"First year of College. There was no way I was still rooming with him, and I kicked him to the basement."

"You didn't kick me out. I left voluntarily." Atticus grunts.

Ashton's room is filled with swimming posters, trophies, and books. His bed is perfectly made with a navy blue blanket, and I can't wait to mess it up. I make my way to the head of the bed, contemplating how to start this conversation. It's not like the messages just started. It's been weeks of this. I grab my phone, swipe it open to all the text messages, and set it down in the middle of the bed.

"I'm sure you don't want me to beat around the bush any longer than I already am."

"Correct. When did it all start?" Atticus moves closer, grabbing the phone.

I watch as he scrolls through all the messages. "The first day of school."

"First day—that was three weeks ago." Ashton snatches the phone, reading the messages. He takes a sharp inhale and stares at me. "You had a panic attack because of this asshole." I watch his blue eyes turn cold.

Maddox takes the phone next, reading, and then his hand freezes.

"Great view the other day. I could make you come too, but with my tongue," he reads."Are you kidding me? He was spying on us in the laundry room?" He throws the phone down, moving to the window.

My eyes snap shut. "He's been spying on me with each of you." I open them, staring at Atticus. "Except once, thank God."

"Just because he didn't send a text doesn't mean he didn't watch us, little grim. From now on, we will keep everything behind closed doors. You have no clue who this could be?"

I shake my head. "No, I already scoped out Cam's room and Liam's." All three growl at me. "Don't need to hear it, and I had to witness some nasty shit in Cam's room during my mission."

"Good, that should teach you a lesson," Maddox fires back.

Oh, it definitely taught me a lesson; bring earplugs next time I scope out bedrooms because I'm never getting caught in that fuckery again. I still can't close my eyes without seeing Juliet sucking Cam's dick. My body shivers thinking about that night.

Atticus hands me his phone. Narrowing my brows at it, I take it. "Use my phone from now on. If this prick messages you again, I'll try to weasel more information from him. I'm not letting him get to you again."

"I don't think that's a good idea. What if he finds out and actually makes a move?" I fidget with my shirt, trying not to let my mind wander further. Atticus places his hands over mine.

"You don't go anywhere alone from now on. Either one of us is with you, or as much as I hate saying this, Spencer." Atticus cringes when he spits Spence's name out.

"He's not a bad guy, and you guys need to spend more time with him. You'll see."

Ashton groans. "Little swan, don't do this to me. I can't deal with more guys around you."

Maddox smiles. "He's not that bad. We've had a few conversations. He thinks highly of our girl."

I should feel relieved that they all know about *Unknown,* except I don't. All I feel is added stress. They have now shoved their way deeper into this situation. I sort of had it handled; it wasn't like this jackass was making personal visits, but those feelings of him watching me today and the other day were unnerving.

Nothing is stopping him from confronting me. For all I know, he's in one of my classes. I need to find something that links us. Or ignore him. The more I interact with him, the more he'll get excited.

"Maybe we should head downstairs before Serena blows a gasket." I climb off the bed. To be truthful, I'm finished with this conversation. I can't handle how all three stare at me like I'm about to break at any second. I probably will if I get another text.

"I'm sure Mom is already blowing up. She went all out on supper, so this is probably killing her." Ashton gives me a provoking grin.

I have a feeling supper is about to get very interesting. I can only hope we make it out in one piece.

Twenty-Seven

Atticus

I'm trying to process everything that Jinx has told us. I wanted to smash her phone after reading all those messages. The way that pervert can go about violating her life without a second thought sends me into a rage. I need to find this asshole before he does something to her. If he can find her phone number, he can find out anything about her. I have so many unanswered questions, and I can't even send him a message, or he'll know I have her phone.

Mother doesn't help my anger issues either; she keeps sending glares to Jinx, and I'm finding it difficult not to yell at her.

"Congratulations again, boys. I'm proud of you." Prescott smiled, holding up his drink.

Kiss ass.

"Yes, boys. I couldn't be more pleased. I'm glad nothing got in your way of winning." Mother sends another glare at Jinx.

Ash rolls his eyes. "Why would there be distractions, Mom?"

Mad and Jinx sit quietly next to each other.

"Don't act like you don't know. You're in a new school. I'm sure there are a lot of new—things there."

Prescott exhales loudly. "Can we just have a nice family dinner without any of this talk? They won a tournament. Can't we celebrate without you mentioning them going to school?"

"Don't start with me, Prescott. It was your idea to send them there. I don't get to see them anymore. If you wanted them to have the same life as your daughter, that's fine, but they are my children."

Jinx goes to open her mouth, and I shake my head. We don't need her in the middle of this fight. We all know it was Mother's idea to ship her off to RWA. It was for the best having Prescott there worked out for the best; at least she got to see her dad every day.

I dig into my mashed potatoes with more force than needed. I knew coming to this dinner was going to be a nightmare.

"Can I say one thing?"

My head snapped up at Jinx, and my heart lurched as she set her fork down.

"Yes, sweetheart," Prescott answers her.

Nervousness prickles run down my spine as she scans the table. One thing about Jinx is that she doesn't hold back when she has something to say, and I can't tell her to shut up right now.

"Serena, I'm sure you are well aware of the family dynamics, correct?" She pauses to look at Mother. "I know it might shock you, but this is called a blended family. You may hate me, but remember that you are disposable. I'm here for the long haul, and I can say whatever I want because I don't live here anymore."

"Odette," Prescott warns her.

"No, Dad. The witch needs to hear this before I leave."

"Watch your mouth." Mother pushes her chair out, slamming her hands on the table. "This is my house, not yours."

Jinx tilts her head, grinning. "Are you sure? Dad, you didn't tell her?"

"Tell me what, Prescott?"

"Odette," he hisses. "Not now."

Ash leans over, whispering in my ear, "Do you know what's going on? Because as much as it's intriguing to watch, I'm a little worried for Jinx."

"I have no fuckin' clue." I look across the table at Mad, and he slowly wraps his hand around the back of Jinx's neck.

"No, Prescott. Tell me what she means."

His fingers clenched around his knife. "It means when I die. Odette is left with everything, including the school. You thought it was your idea to send her there, but it was her destiny. She was always meant to go to RWA."

"I'm sorry, what." Mother clenches her teeth.

"That means you end up with nothing, just like you had when you came into this marriage, Serena," Jinx adds.

I'm speechless. Ravenwood belongs to Prescott? How? I have so many questions. Why weren't we told this when we moved in or enrolled in the school? My brain is working overtime with all this new information that I didn't see the smack coming.

"You watch what you say."

"What the fuck, Mom," Ash yells, pushing his seat back and rushing to Jinx. Mad already has her pulled to her side.

"You lay another hand on my daughter, and you'll be out in the cold." Prescott threatens her, moving in her direction. "I put up with a lot of your garbage, but smacking my child isn't one of them."

Mad moves Jinx out of the way, her cheek red from where Mother had hit her. In all my life, I've never seen her hit anyone. Nor have I heard Prescott talk like that toward her. This entire night has gone to shit.

"I think it's best if we head back to campus," Mad says, breaking the tension.

"You do that. I'll talk with everyone on Monday." Prescott simply dismisses us without a second glance.

Mad and Ash guide Jinx out of the dining room, and I follow behind. I glance back, watching Prescott guide Mother toward the kitchen. I'm not worried; Prescott would never harm her. They have a lot of things to discuss, just like the four of us do.

Being in Jinx's dorm feels like I'm at home. Her scent surrounds me like a blanket for someone who always dresses in black. I wouldn't expect her to smell like a beach, but her coconut smell is refreshing. I watch as she attends to her little raven friend. She can deny everything she wants, but Cinderella should be her new nickname. Even Mad is down on the floor talking to the bird, like a fairy godmother. What in the stars is going on in this dorm room?

I clear my throat. "So, your old man owns the college, and you weren't gonna tell us?"

She sits with her legs spread open, the bird between them. "Listen, Dad, and I made an agreement that no one would know. Can you imagine if everyone found out? I have one friend now. Either I would have a bunch of fakes or enemies. I'm fine with Spence."

"Does he know?"

I swear to God if he knows. I'm gonna lose it.

"Nobody knows, and I feel like shit lying to my best friend. The only one that knows is Florence."

"The hipster secretary," Ash bursts out.

"Yep, it would be kinda weird if I visited the dean often, wouldn't it?" She raises a brow at Ash like he's stupid.

He goes back to playing on his phone. That reminds me; I pull her phone out and scroll through all the messages from this unknown person. Reading through all of them, she even asked if it was Cameron. She asks who it is, and he taunts her, telling her she knows him. In a school this size, that doesn't help. It has to be somebody in our year or the year below us.

"I'm gonna head out for the night."

"You sure? We can all watch a movie in my room." She climbs to her feet, a worried look to her.

I move to her, brushing her hair away from her face. "I'm sure. I'm a little tired after swimming and need some alone time." I pause as I near her mouth, licking my lips. "Don't get me wrong, little grim. I would love to stay, but I don't want to share you right now." I grip her neck, pulling her until our lips meet. Her fingers twist my shirt, drawing me closer. Working my way along her jaw, I tilt her head getting access to her neck; her sweet moans fill the room, and her stomach presses into my hard dick.

I rather feel something else on my dick. Sliding my hands under her ass, I lift her pressing her pussy into my dick. "Fuck, that feels better."

"You sure you don't want to stay?"

I groan into her neck. "Tempting as that pussy is, next time. I just wanted to feel it again."

She chuckles, running her hand down my chest and into my jeans. Her fingertips brush the tip of my dick.

"We could have a quickie."

"No such thing as a quickie, but with the way Ash and Mad look at you, I'm sure they would love to take care of you."

She looks down at them and smiles. Those two need to figure out their shit and fast. Ash has his reason, I get that, but it's not fair that she doesn't know them. She's told us so much. I place her down, giving her one last kiss before I leave her room.

I have some information I need to dig up.

Now that I know Prescott owns this joint, breaking into his computer is a lot easier. And getting into the office will be a breeze tonight. Everyone is out partying at Blackwood, leaving the campus empty. No witnesses.

His passwords couldn't have been more dad-like. I'll give it to him; he sure is proud of Jinx. I open the class list and find all the males. Scrolling through, I start comparing to see who is in her classes; that's the only thing I can think of. It'll be more manageable once I can cross off those that aren't in her classes. I'm not sure how I'll narrow it down even further, but that's a bridge to cross once I get to it.

I print the list and her class list. I have a feeling I'll be up late tonight.

Twenty-Eight

Jinx

The door barely closes behind Atticus before Ashton lifts me over his shoulder.

"I'm gonna have fun with you tonight, Maddox. You joining or what?"

"I'll watch."

Oh, sweet merciful. These guys are going to kill me.

Ashton smacks my ass, making my core clench hard. I clutch the back of Ashton's shirt tight, breathing in that clean scent I love the most. The world spins before landing on my bed, starfish.

"Not how I want you, but it'll work. Get undressed." Ashton's blue eyes dance with amusement.

He watches me as I pull my shirt over my head, leaving me in my lace bralette.

"Ah, shit. Jinx." He snaps open his jeans.

I stand on my bed, unbuttoning my jeans to torment him more. I kick off my shoes. The first one missing Maddox. Who took residence in my armchair in the corner. He gives me a little grin in return.

Ever so slowly, I wiggle my jeans down my hips, bending over. I hear Ashton groan when he sees my cleavage.

Or the lack of.

"Like what you see, Ash?" I ask once I'm in my bra and underwear.

Biting his lip, he kneels on the bed, running a finger under my bra strap. "Little swan, I don't like anything about you." He slides my strap down before going for the other one. "I love everything about you."

My heart is beating so fast that I become breathless from his words. He guides his fingertips over my breast so that my flesh crawls with electricity. I tug his shirt up, wanting to feel his skin against mine. His hands are only off my body briefly before they are back on me, palming every inch of my skin. Digging his hand into my hair, he pulls my head back. His tongue traces my throat, up my chin, and when he reaches my mouth.

"I'm still not going to fuck you, but I will have fun with you." His mouth is hot and demanding, pressing his tongue past my lips. I try to be dominant, but he doesn't have that. Pressing his tongue against mine, he swirls along my tongue before sucking on it.

My body is like melted ice cream in the summer heat, relaxing into the mattress as Ashton presses his body on mine, his hand moving between us, rubbing my aching clit. I pull away, moaning loud and needy.

"In time. Maddox, hand me that candlestick." Ashton pulls my underwear off, spreading my legs wide. "Drenched for me already, and I barely touched you."

Maddox hands him my black candlestick, and he drags it over my stomach. Maddox sits on the bed, getting a better view of the show. The bulge in his pants lets me know he's really enjoying it. I move my hand to his thigh when Ashton rubs the candle along my clit.

"Tell me, little swan. Have you ever fucked yourself since Ace took your virginity?" He dips the candle lower.

"No."

"A first for everything." He slides the candle inside my aching core.

I dig my heels into the bed when he angles it, hitting my g-spot. My fingers dig into Maddox's thigh.

"Do you like this?" He moves faster.

I arch my back, moaning. "Yeah, I like that." My hips flex, moving with him. I whimper when I feel myself getting close.

His fingers move small circles on my clit. A sharp sting has me crying out.

He fucking smacked my clit.

"Please, Ash. I need more," I beg him.

He smacks me again, making me cry out more. "God, you are so irresistible when you make those noises." Pinching my clit, I come, squirting all over him and clenching around the candlestick.

"Ashton, oh God." My body spasms as I come down from my high. When I look at him, he's sucking the candlestick off.

"You taste delectable." Licking his lips, he moves over me, kissing me. I can taste my sweetness on his lips and tongue.

"What about you two?"

"I'm fine," he replies, getting off the bed and heading to the bathroom.

I look over at Maddox. "I'm good, baby." Leaning over, he presses a kiss on my forehead. "It was a great show. Now get some sleep."

Ashton comes back with a fresh set of sheets. "Up you get. I'll change the bedding."

Maddox helps me out of bed, and I scoop Ashton's shirt off the floor. I tug it over my head, swimming in extra fabric.

Ashton grins ear to ear when he sees me. "Looks good on ya."

I stretched the shirt out. I could fit another one of me in it. "It's a little big."

"That's because you're so tiny," Maddox says.

I roll my eyes. "That's because you are all giants compared to me."

"You must get that from your mom," Ashton whispers.

My stomach drops. We never bring up that topic. The only one that does is Dad. I have a hard time knowing it was my fault she died.

"I'm gonna go check on Edgar."

"Jinx, I didn't mean anything by it," Ashton rushes out.

"I know." I leave the bedroom without them following me.

I find Edgar sleeping; so much for getting some cuddles in. I move to my bookshelf, pulling out my photo album. Flipping to the very back, I find the one and only picture I have with my mom. I gently run my finger over her face.

"You look just like her," Ashton spoke softly, sitting to my left and wrapping his arm around my shoulder.

"She's gorgeous, Jinx," Maddox says, sitting to my right, stroking my cheek.

"I only wish I knew her. Every year, it gets harder and harder. There is something you just need to talk about with a mom, and no offense to my dad, but I can't talk about sex with him."

"I think you figured out the whole sex thing, baby." Maddox laughs.

"Shut up." We all fall into laughter because it's true.

Ashton takes my album from me and places it on the table. Before turning back to me, his face goes all serious. "Your mom loves you no matter what, and you need to get it out of your head that you killed her. That didn't happen; things happen during childbirth all the time, and it's no one's fault, okay?"

I nodded, placing a hand to my throat, feeling a lump forming. "It's not that easy."

"No, but every time you get those thoughts in your head, you tell yourself it wasn't your fault and that she loves you. You aren't a jinx," Maddox tells me, his voice falling to a whisper.

They guide me back to bed, where my brain refuses to turn off.

***

"Seriously, Jinx, that's not how this is going to work. You need to follow my rules if you want to survive the year." Atticus glares at me across the room.

"Why are you being such a douche right now?"

He takes a step forward. "Because I didn't ask to be a part of this family, do you think I wanted to move here and get thrown into a house where they talk during suppers about their fun, happy day? Fuck no. I was content with being fatherless."

I shake my head. Maybe he should have thought of that before his mother decided to whore herself out. I still don't understand what I did for him to blow up on me like this. He thinks he has owned me ever since I asked him to get my cello back. Wrongo. You don't.

"If this is for your punishment from Dad, get over yourself. I said I would own up to it."

"You would've liked being the hero, wouldn't you?" He laughs.

"Wow. Someone has a god complex, and it's not me."

He moves fast, pinning me to the couch, pressing his growing dick into my stomach. "I know you want me to, so don't act like you don't. I also know you want my brother and my best friend. What a fucked-up family this would be if it happened. How would you explain this to Daddy?"

I jolt awake, breathing heavily. Pressing my hand to my chest, crap. I try to take a deep breath, but my lungs scream at me. I try to get out of bed, but a lump blocks me.

"Jinx?" Maddox rasps out.

Fuck it, I climb over him, getting a groan when I knee him in the stomach. I topple out of bed, landing on the floor with a thump.

"Shit, Jinx. What the hell." Maddox whips out of bed, lifting me.

"I need my inhaler." I struggle for air. Thankfully, I leave them lying around like candy. He grabs the one on my nightstand. That sweet sound of that puff sends relief to my lungs.

"Tell us what happened, little swan," Ashton says from the comfort of the bed.

Bastard.

"Just a little nightmare involving your brother."

Ashton sits up, narrowing his eyes. "Tell me, now."

I sit in my armchair, burying my head into my hands. Reality is finally hitting me in the guts.

"I think I made a mistake."

"How so?" the words half-died in Ashton's throat.

"What am I going to tell my dad? Oh my God, what if your mom finds out? I can't believe I didn't think of this before I slept with Atticus."

"Okay, none of that." Ashton rushes over, cradling me into his arms. "Listen to me. We are adults, correct?"

"Yes."

"We spent a year living together as step-siblings, then you left and never came back, not even for a Christmas. Can you honestly classify us as step-siblings?"

I give him a dismissive shrug.

"That would be a no, but I don't mind if you call me step bro."

Maddox laughs. "Of course you don't."

"You are such a dog." I laugh.

"It got you to laugh. Can we go back to bed and worry about this tomorrow? We can talk to Ace and see what he has to say—again."

A phone dings, but Ashton steers me back to bed, ignoring it. Whoever it is, it can wait until morning. If it were important, they would call anyway.

Twenty-Nine

Jinx

Waking up with two warm bodies feels amazing, but after that nightmare and realizing that I might have just ruined my relationship with Dad, it has soured my mood for the day. These two haven't even stirred, pissing me off more. I need to get out; maybe a day with Spence is in order.

Climbing over the Maddox lump, I head for the bathroom, turning on the shower. The bathroom fills with steam while I stare at myself in the mirror, watching it fog up and wondering how my life became such a complicated mess.

A gentle knock comes at the door. "Jinx, you doing okay?"

It's nice that Maddox cares so much, but I need some space. I've gone too long by myself. "I'm good. You don't always need to check up on me."

A thump hits the door, his head, I think. "Watch it, baby. I'll still smack your ass raw."

His words only make my core clench. "Shit," I spoke lowly.

His chuckle is the last thing I hear as I step under the water. Dickhead.

When I open the bathroom door, my bedroom is empty. Their voices float in from the kitchen, and Edgar's little squawks. That bird is loved like no other and spoiled beyond his years. I busy myself with grabbing clothes from my closet, hearing a phone ding again. I look around, confused. Then I remembered I had Atticus' phone, and that's not my sound.

The phone sucks me in like a black hole, and dread fills me immediately. Turning the phone on, my stomach clenches tight.

Unknown: You naughty little thing. You didn't think I would figure it out. I'm not that stupid. I knew you would tell on me.

I read the newest message.

Unknown: Odette. Don't ignore me, didn't your mother tell you that's rude? Oops sorry, that's right she's dead. I guess I should rephrase that. Daddy Dean didn't teach you very well, did he?

What the fuck. My handshakes as I try to type out a response.

Me: What do you want from me?!

Unknown: Everything. Can't you tell?

Me: Who are you? Why won't you tell me?

Unknown: Where is the fun in that?

I quickly dial my phone, calling Atticus.

"Jinx."

"He knows you have my phone," I rush out.

"How do you know?"

"Because he just sent me a text."

The line is silent. I pull the phone away to see if I lost the call. "Ace?"

"I'm on my way up. Open the fuckin' door." He hangs up.

I grab a pair of sweatpants and a hoodie. Rushing past the guys, I swing open the door to find a pissed of Atticus.

"I want your door access code." He pushes past me, leaving no room for argument.

"It's my birthday," I yell to the room.

"Um. Whatcha doing here, bro?" Ashton looks at Atticus, confused.

Atticus looks at me, raising his blond brow. I shrug. "I didn't have time to share with the class."

"Share now, Jinx." He growls.

I growl back. "Fine, asshat knows I don't have my phone."

That sends the twins and Maddox into an explosive argument. I simply sit down while they yell at each other. Edgar hops over to me, bending down; I bring him onto my lap to watch the show.

"What the hell does she mean he found her?" Ashton asks.

"Where's the phone? I need to see the messages." Maddox swings around, looking at me.

I point to my bedroom. They can read that shit for themselves. I'm not rereading or retelling it. How *Unknown* knows about my parents is what's eating at me.

"Odette, the fuck." Maddox storms back, the government name. He's pissed.

"Trust me, I know. Atticus, can I see my phone for a sec?"

Without question, he hands it over. That surprises me.

Me: Get to my dorm now.

Pencil: Why is everything okay?

Me: Shit has gone down, and I need to tell you some stuff.

Pencil: I'll be there soon.

I need my bestie here for moral support. Ashton moves behind me, placing his hand on my shoulder massaging my neck.

"I just don't understand how he knew Ace had Jinx's phone."

"My concern is how the hell does he know about my parents."

My door opens, and all three guys are instantly on high alert. Ashton's grip tightens on my shoulder. Spence walks in slowly.

"Um, should I be worried? What's going on?" He nervously asks, stepping further inside.

"Sit. I need to tell you a few things." I point to the couch.

Atticus scoffs, and I shoot him a glare.

"Teeny, you're scaring me. The last time we had a heart-to-heart was because you broke the computer, and you haven't been in my dorm for a long time."

I cringe at the reminder. I'm not allowed to touch his electronics anymore. "It's, um, worse."

"Fuckballs. Lay it on me."

And that's what I do. I tell Spence everything. The good, the bad, and the fuckin' ugly. I feel bad that I lied to him about my dad owning the college, but there are some things I didn't have control over telling others. That was a secret Dad and I made. After telling Serena, I knew it was on the table and if the guys knew. Spence needed to know.

His face pales when I tell him about my stalker friend.

"Why didn't you tell me sooner?"

"Don't take it to heart. She only told us yesterday," Atticus shot back, rolling his eyes.

"Tell me the plan. How are we catching this pervert? How did he know you switched phones in the first place?"

Spence paces the small space, rubbing his chin. He's thinking hard.

"I have no idea. I broke into Prescott's office last night and printed a list of all the male students who are in Jinx's classes. I figured we could cross reference that."

Spence and I both look at Atticus, stunned. "How? I tried hacking into his computer before."

He makes the zipper motion over his lips. "Can't say. The point is, we need to find this asshole before he does something to Jinx."

"Where's the list?"

"Back in the dorm, we can go over it later. What we need is a game plan because I'm not letting you out of my sight."

"Well, I have music with her," Maddox finally speaks.

Ashton pipes up, "I have Business Management."

Atticus watches me. "I have Psych, which is before your class with her, Mad. So I can meet you halfway."

I watch as they figure out everything,

My phone dings and the room falls silent.

I stare at the phone that someone left on the table.

Ashton walks over, picking it up. "It's from him."

"Read it," Atticus demands.

Unknown: Think you can hide behind those walls. Meet me by the food court if you are brave enough.

TO BE CONTINUED...

Ashton
https://mybook.to/BOhM

ALSO BY

A HITMAN'S DUET
MYLES

CARTER

RUSSO MAFIA SERIES
UNBROKEN

UNBEARABLE

UNDENIABLE

STRANGERS OF EASTWOOD
STRANGERS OF THE NIGHT

STRANGERS OF THE TOWN

STRANGERS OF THE CROWD

RAVENWOOD ACADEMY
ATTICUS

ASHTON

MADDOX

STANDALONE
CHRISTMAS UNWRAPPED

PAINFULLY MERRY

SWEET DREAMS

About the Author

Hello, loves! I'm a Canadian romance writer who's all about the steamy and dark stuff. Horror books, movies, and music? Yes, please! I have a little true crime obsession, but I'll just call it research and pretend it's normal.

If you crave love stories that push the limits of lust, trust, and desire, you've come to the right place.

Follow me for exclusive sneak peeks, giveaways, and behind-the-scenes glimpses into my writing process. And if you want to keep up with my latest releases or connect on social media.

Let's dive into the shadows together, darlings.

www.ingramcontent.com/pod-product-compliance
Lightning Source LLC
Chambersburg PA
CBHW061119310726

48974CB00002B/601